Praise for _Flight_

"Kornher-Stace masterfully w
romp that is somehow both nail-bitingly suspenseful
and tenderly cozy, as if the authors of _How to Win the
Time War_ had decided to set _The Boxcar Children_ in _Snow
Crash_'s tongue-in-cheek hyper-capitalist dystopia. _Flight
& Anchor_ is a stunning achievement."
—Maria Dong, author of _Liar, Dreamer, Thief_

"A character study in possibility, heartache, sacrifice, and
friendship. Wonderful."
—Max Gladstone, author of _Last Exit_

"Nicole Kornher-Stace's _Flight & Anchor_ pulls you along
with the speed of a dystopian freight train. Taking the
weaponized childhoods of kids like Ender and blending
in a touch of Hanna-style rebellion against the mother
organization, Kornher-Stace draws you into a story not
only of survival but of calculated surrender to drive the
best possible outcome."
—Kimberly Unger, author of _Nucleation_

"_Flight & Anchor_: what a feat of adrenaline, friendship,
loyalty, fraught circumstance, and fun! Nicole Kornher-Stace deftly—exquisitely—balances the lightness of
classic runaway-child books (_Boxcar Children_! _From the
Mixed-Up Files of Mrs. Basil E. Frankweiler_!) with the
savagery of survival-in-the-wilderness books (_Hatchet_!

Robinson Crusoe!) to entertaining and harrowing effect."
—C. S. E. Cooney, author of *Saint Death's Daughter*

"Kornher-Stace's nail-biting novella, full of Easter eggs for fans of her expanding universe, keeps us grounded in stakes that are both world-shattering and movingly human."
—Mike Allen, Shirley Jackson Award–nominated author of *Aftermath of an Industrial Accident*

"Kornher-Stace finds a perfect balance between human childhood and otherworldliness by making us fall for the myth and propaganda surrounding 06 and 22 while also making them deeply human, if only deep down. A burning ember of humanity in the midst of overwhelming propaganda."
—*Bookish Brews's Reviews*

Flight & Anchor

Nicole Kornher-Stace

Also by Nicole Kornher-Stace

Desideria (2008)
Archivist Wasp (2015)
Latchkey (2018)
Firebreak (2021)
Jillian vs Parasite Planet (2021)

FLIGHT & ANCHOR

NICOLE KORNHER-STACE

TACHYON
SAN FRANCISCO

Flight & Anchor
© 2023 by Nicole Kornher-Stace

Interior and cover design by Elizabeth Story

Tachyon Publications LLC
1459 18th Street #139
San Francisco, CA 94107
415.285.5615
www.tachyonpublications.com
tachyon@tachyonpublications.com

Series editor: Jacob Weisman
Editor: Jaymee Goh

Print ISBN: 978-1-61696-392-7
Digital ISBN: 978-1-61696-393-4

Printed in the United States by Versa Press, Inc.

First Edition: 2023
9 8 7 6 5 4 3 2 1

For all the readers, who keep giving me a reason

1.

ONE COLD NIGHT, two children stand in front of a coffee shop. Snow blows all around them, and they are badly dressed for it. A boy and a girl, the barista thinks, noticing them through the plate glass. Young enough or short enough that the window-paint lettering COFFEE, retouched just that morning by the barista themself in blue to match the blue chalk on the sidewalk chalkboard, arcs over both their cold-huddled heads like a monochrome rainbow.

Strange clothing, the barista notes. The one they think might be a girl is in an oversize lime-green blazer, the maybe-boy in a white lab coat, like a tiny pharmacist. Both blazer and lab coat are buttoned the whole way up, but the blazer only goes so far. Beneath it, the girl's got on what looks like a simple dark shirt that buttons up the front. No winter gear to speak of. No real coats, even. Snow in their hair. Window light pools around them: soft, buttery, looking much warmer than it is.

The barista checks the time on their lenses. Four minutes 'til closing. Quiet this time of evening, usually. Storm like this, the place is dead.

A normal day, they'd be finishing up wiping down the counters now. Flipping the door sign—like the chalkboard, a symptom of how terminally old-school their boss is—to CLOSED. Walking the six blocks to the checkpoint, then the two blocks home. Tilting their head back, from time to time, to let the app on their lenses show them where the stars would be, if the sky weren't wall-to-wall snow and smog instead.

Frozen with rag in hand, though, they're just standing there. Watching these two weird kids devour that yellow light with their eyes.

Nine years old or so, the barista reckons. Then reconsiders. It's the look on the children's faces that's lifting years off them, peeling them back to something less worldly, less certain. It's in the way the upper half of the girl's body is oscillating toward and away from the door, one indecisive degree at a time, while her feet, in their no doubt seasonally inappropriate attire, do not move. In how the boy holds himself in perfect, ready stillness, in a way that reminds the barista of nothing so much as their cat, facing down a spider, unsure which of them is the hunter and which the prey.

Eleven, maybe. Twelve at most. In any case too young for this shit. Unsupervised. Underdressed. Three hours into an expected all-night nor'easter. They look like they're wearing half a Halloween costume apiece. And not the good kind. The kind you slap together out of stuff from your parents' closets and basements when you can't afford the ones at the party store.

The snow is coming down in big clumpy flakes now.

When it hits the kids' faces, it takes an alarmingly long time to melt.

In hindsight, the barista will wonder why it took them so long to act. Unpack, in bullet points, as part of a whole minute-by-minute replay of everything they should have done instead. Rationalize, albeit feebly.

- Because the children weren't visibly injured.
- Because the barista has their implant set to alert them if there's a bioweapon in the air and it hadn't gone off in days.
- Because one of the best parts of this job is how it's way out on the edge of the Stellaxis half of the city, just a couple of blocks from the Greenleaf one, near enough to the little strip of demilitarized zone that, beyond a few small skirmishes, this street hasn't seen real combat since October.
- Because, due to the above, there was no quantifiable threat from which the kids need rescuing. Just two kids, ogling a warm haven from the cold.

Because the real answer makes less sense.

Because the real answer doesn't land as a thought, not a fully formed one anyway. It's more of a catch in the barista's breath every time this girl so much as shifts from foot to foot, or brushes the snow from her face, or shoves her hands deeper in her pockets, and every time the boy pointedly does none of these things. It hits as a tiny chemical shock, like getting slapped on the back of the skull. *Danger*, it's telling them. *Run*.

The barista gives this due consideration. Then, deliberately, over the mental alarms this raises, they push it carefully away. They're children on their own in the snow. Maybe they're looking at the barista alone in the shop and thinking they can clean out the register and get gone before the barista can blink up a security patrol on their lenses. At their age—hell, at older—the barista would've done the same. Endless war fucks with you like that. Pares down your options to what starts to look a lot like one single, inevitable, ill-advised point.

The barista puts down the rag. Whatever the fuck this is, it's not happening on their watch. They march across the warmth of the room and haul open the door. Two faces snap to them, too quickly, raising little hairs on the back of their neck. The word *vampires* skips unbidden across the surface of the barista's mind. *Have to be invited in.*

But no. These are just a couple of cold kids who've clearly had a hell of a day. Close up, the blazer and pharmacist coat are snow-damp but clean, a faint chemical smell wafting off them that the barista at first mistakes for the perfume of dryer sheets—then realizes they can't quite identify. The kids themselves: also clean. Well-fed. At a glance, no signs of chronic dehydration. This isn't life for them, then. At least not yet. Just a misadventure. The kind that gets the *mis-* tacked on in hindsight, best the barista can tell. Plenty of those in their past. They know the signs.

In the children's proximity, the barista's lenses remain silent. Nothing airborne and deadly has seeped into their weird Halloween-costume attire, waiting to be unleashed on the shop's interior. The barista blinks up a quick weapons-check interface—not exactly retail worker standard-issue, but one can only hear so many on-the-job horror stories before going to a cousin of a friend of a friend with a month's worth of tips for a small software upgrade—and, of course, the kids aren't packing. Not so much as a rusty junk-shop pocketknife or a few inches of sharpened rebar, and that's maybe most surprising of all. They're out here wandering around in what could at any minute renew its status as a conflict hot zone, and they're defenseless.

So the barista props the door open with one hip. Tilts their head in toward that delicious drench of coffee-scented warmth. *Letting the heat out,* Rach—the owner, Rachel, the barista's boss—would say. But Rach doesn't stay for closing, and nothing fills the day-old bakery basket like a big-ass storm, and, these kids can wait for whoever they belong to just as well out of the snow as in it, and if the barista gets back to their apartment a little later than usual, honestly so what.

The kids pause to assess the barista, straddling the doorway in their jeans and undercut and apron like it's a magic portal and they've got one sneaker in each world and finding both options underwhelming. The question of the kids' footwear remains a mystery for now, as both have white plastic Comforts of Home shopping bags tied over what at least, thankfully, do look like decent boots. There is snow in their eyelashes. The barista's pretty sure they've been standing outside the window for only five to six minutes, max. Could track their prints back behind them, before the snow dusts them over. See where they've been. Who's looking to follow after.

But that could be anywhere. Anyone. And they're here now, and who knows what's behind them. Some paths are best left unwalked, or unrepeated. It's a big city, and not all of it as nice as Rach's place. Not nearly.

All at once, both kids straighten as something passes between them invisibly, and despite themself, the barista shudders. Something's off about their movement, something dreamlike, something the barista has seen before, grasps after, glances off.

It won't be until tomorrow that they'll realize, hands shaking hard enough to drop the stack of to-go cups they're carrying out from storage, what exactly it is they're looking at. By which point it will be too late to either help or hinder them. Both hypotheticals will strike them, suddenly, as absolutely laughable.

They'll tell the story of this night for years to come. They live and work in a city that's been at civil war with itself for decades and this, right here, is probably the closest they have ever come to death.

For now, whatever this weird feeling is, it lasts only that one nanosecond. Then they're kids again and cold and hungry, and they're tracking grimy snow onto the just-cleaned tile, and the barista sighs and flips the sign to CLOSED behind them, and then goes to fetch a mop.

2.

IN THE LIGHT, at a table, snow steadily melting off them and puddling around their chair legs, the barista's earlier observations are proven correct: two healthy-looking, well-fed, clean children of twelve or so. Each sits before a giant paper cup of coffee with enough flavoring syrup to give their grandkids cavities, enough soywhip on top that they'll have to tunnel into it with plastic spoons. The day-old bakery basket sits between them, full of cellophane-wrapped muffins and oversize cookies. Couple of brownies. The barista makes the executive decision that the brownies will be their dinner if the kids don't inhale them first.

When the children are sufficiently hopped up on sugar to (hopefully) drop their weirdly considerable guard, the barista will ferret out their secret. For now, they rock their chair back on two legs in the exact way that used to drive their mother up the wall, as if to say to these kids: *see, I'm not so old. You can trust me. I'm one of the good ones.*

But the kids just sit there awkwardly, not appreciating the elegance and solidity of the barista's plan.

There's another pause, like they're conferring. It's less weird under the lights, at least—looks less like telepathy and more like they're chatting over their implants like anyone else.

"Nice jackets," the barista ventures. Gestures toward the hooks by the door. Old-school's not so bad, they figure. Company coffee shop wouldn't have those. Or baked goods that weren't primarily cellulose and flavoring. Or a living, breathing barista to offer a couple of runaways a basket of same, gratis, instead of having already called in some company cops on a loitering charge. Old-school's pretty fucking great, actually, all things considered. "If you want to hang them up over there to dry . . ."

They trail off. The kids have gone guarded again. Their arms tighten against their sides, like those ridiculous jackets are about to be taken from them by force.

Not that, then.

A moment passes. Another. Then the kids reach into their pockets and come out with a handful of loose change apiece, actual, physical metal coins like maybe one customer a day pays with. It's a good way to tell at a glance when a person's implant's been locked out or otherwise disabled, infrequent enough that Rach keeps saying she doesn't need to waste the counter space on a register anymore, not when upward of ninety-five percent of customers blink over their coffee money to the smart surface of the counter directly.

None of which is easily reconciled with how the kids are pretty obviously conversing with each other over their implants *now*.

The barista waves this off before they can start counting their cash out on the tabletop.

"My treat. I'm Cass, by the way," Cass says, tapping their nametag like it hasn't already been evaluated, inventoried, classified, along with every thread of their clothing and every pore of their face. Can't shake the feeling that they've passed some kind of test, just in having successfully coaxed two half-frozen kids in out from the cold. That the fact of them, here, staring at their cooling coffees while the storm rains off them, is test number two.

Is it a hospital, what they smell like? No, that's also wrong. This is going to bug Cass for a while. Like being unable to place where you've seen an actor in a movie. They *hate* that.

The kids look at them like Cass is a trap they're working out how to disarm. Cass, who remembers being a shy child themself, smiles, reaches for a brownie, peels back the cellophane, and takes a big, slightly-too-crumbly bite. The kids watch Cass chew, swallow. Cass can't tell if it's that the kids are hungry or or that they're trying to figure out whether they're about to be poisoned, waiting to see what happens when that sticky mouthful hits Cass's guts.

Meanwhile, the boy is pushing his pile of coins across the table resolutely. "We can pay," he says. It's the first that either of them has spoken. Voice like a person passing a checkpoint ID scan, trying to duck their face into the collar of their shirt, never mind that it's the implant, not the face, that's being scanned. One hundred percent instinctual, and one hundred percent a gesture too old for a child of twelve. He wears it like the coat: outsize. Cass files this away. "Take it."

Cass shakes their head. "Sorry, kid. Already closed the register. Besides, we're running a special today. Free coffee and muffins to the last two customers of the evening."

They track the boy's left eyebrow as it quirks up by about a half millimeter. Shakes his head. It's another tiny, tiny movement, planned and executed with what looks to be a surprising amount of concentration. For all that the girl's weird grace of motion grates at Cass's backbrain, the boy's painstaking exertion of control over his is worse. This kid moves like he's holding two leashes with sleeping tigers at the end of them, and both are *this* close to waking up.

"We can pay," he says again. It isn't that his teeth are gritted. It's more that his whole person is. "How much?"

Like the prices aren't on the board above the counter, in clear line of sight from his side of the table. Like this kid's pile of change amounts to anything close to the cost of one lone small black drip coffee, let alone the sixteen-dollar confection Cass has concocted, times two. At a glance, what's come out of the boy's pocket is about seventy cents, mostly pennies, encrusted with sidewalk grime, still wet with snow.

"Sure," Cass says, conceding. "Fine." They reach over with two outstretched fingers, plant the tips on the tails of two pennies, drag them back to Cass's side of the table.

Cass watches the boy pocket the remainder, apparently satisfied. "There," they say. "Commerce concluded."

Very weird urge to fake-spit on their palm, hold it out for a handshake. All the weirder because Cass is not remotely confident it would be taken as the joke intended. "Now drink up. That's real coffee. Better when it's warm." Then, doubtfully: "Is the flavoring strong enough?" Cass is a fucking superlative barista, and they know the best way to a child's heart is with a pure, clean, massive hit of glucose straight to the bloodstream. As such, each kid got two pumps of salted caramel and two of white mocha.

Politely, the girl sips, then the boy. Cass watches the first jolt of sugar visibly cross the blood–brain barrier, trailing a bright-burning comet tail of dopamine in its wake. The kids' postures relax, fractionally.

"So I'm Cass," Cass says again. They put on a silly voice, because there's no other way to do this. "And *whooom* do I have the pleasure of addressing?"

Cass can feel the glance the kids don't exchange. It rides the air like ozone before a thunderstorm. The girl opens her mouth, then closes it, then pointedly busies herself with another sip. Soywhip on her upper lip. She licks it off. The trick-of-the-light weirdness a minute ago has vanished. They're just kids, Cass decides. Obviously. Kids with something to hide, or kids hiding from something, or both. Cass studies their faces for evidence of violence, finds none. Won't get further unless they convince them to lose those jackets. Which looks increasingly unlikely. Or, for that matter, the gloves they suddenly realize both kids are wearing. Some kind of weirdly high-end-looking synthleather. Way too thin for winter. They seem useless for most anything. Even to call them decorative would be a stretch, and they don't square with the lime blazer and pharmacist coat in any way that Cass can puzzle out. Plain, utilitarian, but thin, like a second skin. Stolen? But the fit is perfect. And they *match*. Nothing about these kids adds up.

Cass glances up, brow furrowed, finds two pairs of eyes trained on them like headlights. Rolls their sleeves up, realizing it's nerves that make them do that. For what might track the kids here? Or the kids themselves? Cass leaves that carefully unprobed. And understands, in quick succession, two things: that the girl is taking in the newly bared skin of their arms with full attention, and that she would do the same with anything unfamiliar she was shown.

Self-conscious, Cass rolls both arms downward, the inner softs of them against the tabletop. It isn't that these kids seem threatening, exactly. But it isn't *not* that, either.

"You can never truly," the girl says, and it's a blinking moment of confusion before Cass understands she's reading their ink aloud, the tattoo that snakes down from the crook of their elbow to bracket the bone of their wrist. Cass pivots their arm around, letting the girl read the rest. "Know a person. You can never truly know a person."

Her eyes reach back up, fishhook Cass's gaze. A question in them, but Cass is unsure what it is, and the girl doesn't elaborate. Instead she gives a little jolt, like someone's kicked her under the table. Cass tracks to the boy, but nothing. Face like stone. Whatever he did, the girl ignores it. She slides the day-old basket toward herself, selects a banana nut muffin. Passes the basket to the boy, who leaves it there.

All at once, unasked for, Cass realizes who these kids remind them of. Through no physical similarity of their own, really. A while back, some kid Rach's sister, Bea, used to babysit went missing. Looked nothing like these two—gods know Bea showed Cass the photos, more than once—but something about their age, their vulnerability, their lack of supervision in a full-on blizzard. Their plausible *missingness.*

And Cass knows as well as anyone that appearances can change, be changed. If there's something looking for the old you, the one who ran. The you who's dead now, metamorphosed into someone who wears lime blazers and lab coats like protective camouflage. Where'd the old you go? Who knows. Never heard of them.

It's probably nothing. It's almost definitely nothing. How many kids go missing in this city? The war's raged on for years. Buildings come down every day. Kids slip through the cracks every day. Rach's community corkboard in the entryway, all those MISSING PERSON faces staring out, incongruously happy photos for how *gone* they are, more crowded every day. Bea wouldn't be the first person to have trouble moving on from bad news, nor the last.

They're nobody Cass recognizes from that sea of corkboard faces. Which means nothing.

Still, they're a long moment deliberating. In their experience, there are two kinds of lost. *Better if found* and *better if mistaken for dead.* And until Cass knows which one they're looking at, they're caught, wheels spinning. A lot of bad shit out there. Bea's *someone is stealing the children from the bombed-out wreckage of their homes* conspiracy theory doesn't exactly hold water—they're accounted for when they get into the company ambulances, they're cared for until their families can be found, that's public knowledge—but on the other hand there are a lot of dark alleys out there. A lot of desperate people. Cass has seen folks who'd kill these two for those fancy gloves alone. Let alone the boots.

"Look," Cass tells the kids. "Wherever you were headed out there, you'll never make it in this. Why don't you sleep here tonight? I'll stay with you," they blurt into the ensuing silence, valiantly. "Keep a watch." For what, they have no idea, but the ice wall of the kids' silent regard thaws another degree, which Cass takes as a win. Warming to it in turn, they gesture to the back corner, where various comfy chairs and a single couch reside, rescued from various sidewalks over the years by Rach and deepcleaned generally by a double-masked and afterward-thoroughly-disinfected Cass. "Nobody can see back there from outside. The counter's in the way."

Not sure whether the couch folds out into a bed, and a little apprehensive of what it'll look like in there if it does, but Cass is game to try. Failing that, there's always the cushions from the comfy chairs. Vague memories of blanket forts fade into mind, just shy of focus. There aren't any blankets here, and Cass doesn't want to leave these two alone in order to fetch some from their apartment, and something about inviting them *back* to their place sits strange with them, like they'll wake to find two weird kids floating just below the ceiling, staring down at Cass with holes for eyes.

But what they *can* do is crank the heat and apologize to Rach in the morning. She'll understand. And even if she doesn't, Bea will side with them no question. Cass's impression is that Bea would take in every stray kid in this city if there was the slightest crumb of a sliver of a fraction of a chance that one of them would know what happened to the one she lost.

Cass shrugs a shoulder in the general direction of the back room, where the lost and found is. Just a cardboard box of abandoned coats and hats, the odd lost glove. Maybe just about enough stuff there to make a nest to fit two midsize twelve-year-old kids. Not clean, at least not recently, but whatever's in that box has been sitting there long enough that whatever germs are on it must have died, right? And if one of the coats and things had picked up some biohazard in a pinned-down zone, Cass reckons their implant would've noticed it shedding interface scramblers or hallucinogens or whatever by this point.

Cass is reversing toward the back room, both eyes on the kids' table, like any second they might break and scatter into the night, or vanish. "Let me just—"

Already pulling up their contacts on their lenses, telling their implant to initiate a chat.

Bea doesn't respond. In a few years, this will be normal for her, as she'll be serving a three-year implant lockout, having gone down on a terrorism charge (purifying rainwater, giving the extra away in the camps). Tonight, though, she's just trying to get better sleep, and part of her multipronged approach involves taking her lenses out at 8 p.m. sharp.

Not that Cass knows this. "Here," they call out, pushing the lost-and-found box through the door with one foot so that it skids across the newly mopped floor and comes to a stop by the girl's left leg. For no reason in particular, they have the sudden and distinct impression that the girl had been about to reflexively shoot out a foot to stop the box midslide, kept still through force of will alone, for no reason that Cass can begin to guess at.

The girl is smiling now. At Cass. Full wattage. It puts Cass uncomfortably in mind of a video they saw a while ago of an octopus changing its coloration in the blink of an eye to match its surroundings. *Look*, this smile seems to say, *normal kid here doing normal kid things*. Protective camouflage to hide from predators.

Or lure in prey.

Almost as an afterthought, the girl reaches her booted foot toward the box and hooks it in. The smile is, if anything, brighter now.

Cass realizes they're staring. Stops. Shakes it off. Smiles back. They're not sure what kind of trauma they're looking at here, but something's very, vry wrong. Whatever's been done to these two, they wear it more heavily than they think, and it's been inked on them in a language Cass doesn't know how to read.

But Bea maybe can.

"Take a look," they suggest brightly. "See what you can use for blankets."

Kids thus busied, Cass tries a direct call, implant-to-implant, and this time Bea picks up.

"Listen," they say, without so much as a hello. "You remember that kid you were looking for?"

Another thing Cass does not know: even in the next room as they are, even whispering as Cass is, even with the door pulled partway shut, Cass ducking behind it, one hand rifling through a new shipment of coffee beans for white noise—the kids can hear them loud and clear.

When Cass emerges from the back room with un-ambiguous marching orders from Bea—*I'll be there in twenty minutes, just hold them there, sit on them if you have to*—the shop's empty. Kids, coffees, coats, contents of the day-old bakery basket, Cass's other brownie and all: gone.

Three things remain to prove to Cass that they didn't hallucinate the past half hour.

The puddles of mucky snowmelt on the floor.

The pile of coins in the day-old basket.

The words THANK YOU spelled out on the tabletop, in soywhip, with a fingertip.

3.

Through the falling snow, the kids walk and walk. They're better dressed for winter now. Each is missing one plastic shopping bag from one boot, but in exchange, 06, the girl, is carrying a plastic shopping bag full of cellophane-wrapped day-old baked goods, and 22, the boy, is carrying another one stuffed with all the extra coats and hats they couldn't quite manage to layer on. Their boots are waterproof already. That's not what the bags were for. It's more that their boots—along with the rest of their uniforms—might be *recognized*. The blazer and lab coat helped a little. Maybe. The lost-and-found box, they agree, helps more. It even had a pair of sunglasses, dark oversize ones, big enough to hide the whole top half of 06's face. With those on, with 22's hair pulled down over his eyes and trapped there under a slouchy hat, with scarves wrapped around their mouths and chins, with their uniforms—all but that one boot apiece—entirely concealed, they feel more or less invincible. Which, by many metrics, they practically are. But not in the way that matters here.

The question of the coat and blazer was the source of some argument a few days ago, when 06 first stole them from the Director's office closet and hid them under the mattress of her cot, there to await the auspicious moment, yet to be discovered, when 06 and 22 could make a break for it.

22's argument: the Director will notice. There are cameras everywhere. Sentry bots. Human guards. The mattress is too thin to hide two coats. Etc.

06's rebuttal: in that case, she'll hide one, 22 will hide the other. Problem solved.

22's prediction: there will be two kidskins hanging from the Director's wall before the week is out.

06's counter prediction: not if we're gone by then, there won't.

Which, of course, was the whole plan anyway. To be gone. To flee. To never so much as think of looking back. Almost four years in, life in the facility, unwanted to begin with, had been scrubbed clean of all its novelty and adventure, all the way down to the dangerous truth of its bones, which was: 06 and 22, along with 05 and 08 and 33 and all the rest of them, had been kidnapped.

(*We'll go to the police,* 22 suggested, on the vague recollection of enough daytime TV to know that this is a thing that daytime-TV people meet with success at doing. *The police have the company logo on their uniforms,* 06 countered, not incorrectly. *They're not on our side.*)

So they don't really have a solid plan. Their old homes, while missed, are recognized as dead ends, as just plain dead. They were dragged from the bombed-out rubble of them personally. They're naive, not stupid. They know there's nothing to go back to.

Nostalgia should have been drugged and beaten out of them by now, but it clings tighter than even the Director can claw loose. They miss their families. Their old homes. Even if they know they're gone, obliterated, never to be returned to. Families: dead. Past lives: erased. They were plucked from the war as eight-year-old orphans, refashioned, reinserted. One engagement to their names already, although that was more or less a glorified parade, something Marketing cooked up and the Director had no choice but to sign off on, even though her professional opinion was and still is that it was a PR stunt prematurely deployed. But Marketing's means suit her ends for the most part: already celebrity builds around the operatives, stacked like bricks to wall them in. Weapons in someone else's fight. Commodities in someone else's product line.

Whose, though? They're twelve and unworldly and unsure. The CEO who owns them is someone they've seen on newsfeeds, maybe, around a kitchen table in an apartment in that old vanished life.

Not the Director's fight, they know that much at least. Someone else's. Someone for whom she's a kind of go-between. Someone more important than anyone in the facility. Someone on the higher floors of the building. Someone aboveground, they imagine, with windows that let in the sun. Maybe one of the strangers who arrive in the facility from time to time, surrounded by assistants armed with candy, to watch the children at lessons, at sparring practice, taking breakfast in the dining hall, feigning sleep beneath the camera's eye.

While the Director and her team scurry fretfully around them, wearing that kicked-dog expression all eleven remaining children recognize, not from the Director's face but from one another's.

In any case, someone who can fight their own stupid war without any help from 06 and 22. Not anymore. They're out. They're free. They've removed themselves from the equation. They're striding through that frigid night like they own it, coughing gloriously in the unfamiliar nonrecycled air, as a million, million snowflakes swirl like tiny, aggrieved ghosts around them. The augments in their eyes were expensive enough, high-tech enough, that if they put their heads way back and squint just so, they can just about pretend to see the stars.

4.

THREE YEARS, ten months, and seventeen days, along with a couple billion dollars, have been spent on these children's optimization. Each can take on a fifteen-ton mech in single combat. Survive a week without water, a month without food. Hear sounds beyond a human's range, an elephant's, a dog's. Read ten-point font at three hundred paces away without squinting. Run laps around this city, their legs so fast that to bystanders they blur.

That said, they are also twelve-year-old children, and they've had a very exciting day. Back at the facility, sugar and caffeine are both strictly controlled substances: banned, except for the Director's cookie stash, which is doled out strategically for lessons excelled, treatments uncried at, naughty behaviors promptly tattled upon to the appropriate authorities, etc. Apart from that, it's a whole-foods diet designed by the best nutritionist that company money can buy. Lots of protein, lots of greens, lots of supplemental vitamins, and the occasional nutrient-paste smoothie.

Tonight, though, 06 and 22 chugged their coffees straight out the door so as not to have to carry them, and those four pumps of flavoring syrup apiece aren't letting them down gently. They crash like meteorites. They're dead on their feet, boots dragging through the drifting snow, elbowing each other to stay awake when they stumble off the sidewalk and careen into a vacant lot between two abandoned, bombed-out warehouse-looking buildings.

The plan, insomuch as they'd devised one, had been to make it out beyond the city limits, into a little patch of distant scraggly forest a few miles away, across open ground. They know it's there: one time 06 spotted it from the roof when the smog lifted, dragged 22 up seventy-six flights of stairs to bear witness to her find. Picturing this safe haven is what's planting 06's right foot before her left one now, over and over. She holds it in her mind, like the last mouthful of water in the canteen.

06's mental version of that green patch in the middle distance: unclear. She remembers a garden, something like a garden, in the apartment she grew up in. Just a few pots on a fire escape. Tiny tomatoes. Blue flowers. Some sharp-smelling green thing that her parents used to have her pinch leaves from, put in pizza sauce. Its name, like so many details of those years, lost now. Eaten by the facility. Deleted. Or rather: overwritten. Her memory feels like a puzzle solved in pencil, then carefully erased, so the next kid can have a turn with the same page. She used to have to do that, share like that, back in day care when she was tiny. Unfair that the facility lets her keep that useless memory and not, for instance, the details of her mother's face.

22's mental image of their destination: less clear

even than hers, and absolutely less optimistic. Then why is he out here, in this storm, instead of snug beneath a standard-issue blanket, while the ceiling speakers pipe in soothing sleep-time tunes? One of the first strokes of genius the Director had was to pair up the children to keep an eye on each other, report back to her and her army of guards and doctors and sentries and medbots, etc., when part of her project goes and does something off script. She's budgeted a *lot* on cameras and spying smart surfaces, and the children's implants record everything they do, but if the Director knows anything about children, it's that they're sneaky. Case in point. The implants' recordings are only worth as much as whoever's at the facility watching the readouts for anomalies, second by second, hour by hour. After the children have been put to bed, 8 p.m. sharp, there's no one.

(Night shift surveillance was an early budget cut, an oversight the Director will correct before tomorrow night's lights-out. Perhaps sentry bots this time, the Director muses. Cheaper, and they won't commit the tactical error of mistaking the operatives as children to be pitied, taught jokes, smuggled candy via pockets, etc. *You learn best from your mistakes*, the Director's mother always used to tell her. *Don't be afraid to make them.*)

(Easy for her to say, the Director will consider in the morning, blood pressure spiking dangerously as the news reaches her that two-elevenths of the remainder of her proj ect have somehow up and disafuckingppeared. *She* doesn't live in terror of having her funding revoked, her project terminated. Mistakes, from inside the

Director's shoes, inside the Director's office, seated behind the Director's nameplate, with the public relations people peering down at the Director from their lofty height for answers, are not so easily bounced back from. In the middle of the first big marketing push, no less. Each surviving child's merchandising budget is more than the past five years' salary of every single person on the Director's team combined. The IP going rogue will not end well for anyone, but the Director's the one, ultimately, who let slip the leash, let all that money stroll right out the goddamn door.)

So it's possible that 22 is here to gather intel on 06's misbehavior. Keep eyes on her in the Director's stead. Return victorious. A model operative. An extension of the Director's will. Lauded. Praised. As many cookies as a twelve-year-old kid can eat. Etc.

That is certainly the hope on which the Director's future hangs, once she realizes exactly who is gone. At first, her fears will run more along the lines of: kidnapping. Sabotage. Intellectual property theft. A mole, a spy, a double agent, a businessperson of some kind. Pilfering the company's best weapon. Taking it apart. Seeing what makes it tick. Analyzing how to replicate it for the other side, or worse: the highest bidder. All this swirling in the Director's gut, the whole ride in to work.

Learning who exactly went missing, she'll laugh. Confusing the hell out of the near-tears tech who wasn't on shift to man the implant readouts but feels the role of scapegoat settling on his shoulders all the same. Slow-motion review of the nighttime cameras will confirm it:

from the boys' dormitory and the girls', respectively, by the glow of the night-light, one stealthy small body subtracting itself. Later still, upon analysis, it will be determined that the hallway sentry bots didn't clock the fleeing children because they moved too fast to trip the sensors in the first place.

The Director's not sure whether to kick herself for this or pat herself on the back.

Still, as long as she can keep a lid on this until 06 and 22 can be retrieved, she's not too worried. She's known these children for four years now, can see clearly the way this will play out. Rebellious 06, sounding her leash's length as usual. High sharp contrast to 22's historical lack of outright insubordination, which the Director is not yet aware she mistakes—chronically thus far, fatally a few years hence—for obedience.

They'll return to her. They're bound to. If not via a shared decision, then by virtue of 22 coercing or compelling 06 back to the fold. They have no resources. No contacts. No safety net. It's much of why they were chosen in the first place, picked from death's pocket, upcycled from their orphanhood, taken under the Director's wing to be reborn. They have no family. No friends. Nowhere, in short, to go.

She gives them twenty-four hours max before they come skulking back. And then 22 will be rewarded, while of 06—the instigator, surely, there's no doubt in the Director's mind—she will make an example the others will not soon forget.

But this is all tomorrow, after the blizzard has spent

itself against the city and lumbered away to the south, leaving all the evidence of years-long corporate civil war—checkpoints, barricades, burned-out vehicles, and all—blanketed in white. After 06 and 22 stumble sugar-dazed and sleep-drunk through the open gate into that vacant lot and find, first, that the buildings on three sides provide a kind of windbreak from the storm, enticing them farther in; second, thus lured, that there is an abandoned gray-blue company shipping container nestled in a corner, the silver of its starry company logo nearly overgrown by pavement weeds and rust; and third, that while it may be locked with a company lock, 06 and 22's company hands are stronger.

5.

INSIDE, the shipping container is cold but empty. The rust hasn't yet chewed through the ceiling. Apart from the snow the children track in with them, the floor is dry. Dark inside, pitch-dark, but nothing the augments in their eyes can't handle. There's a little pile of dry leaves and fast-food wrappers in the corner. A squirrel nest, they guess, just clutching straws from the quicksand of their memories, but honestly they've no idea.

So they didn't make it to the woods. How far have they gotten? Unasked for, their implants display the path they've walked. Neon-blue lines, overlaid on a grid of streets as seen from overhead. 06 ignores hers, but 22 lends his careful study, tightening the corners of his eyes in analysis.

The operatives' ability to gauge distances with razor accuracy has, at this point in their optimization, far outpaced their ability to contextualize that data. The distance that they've traveled is displayed in meters, but 22 doesn't know how to translate that to the miles of trudging he feels in his bones. Still, that blue line isn't anywhere near as long as he would've expected for how cold they are, how tired. He pictures it as a wire tightening, dragging them back bodily, fingertips gouging furrows in the street.

A glance back toward 06 for reassurance, but she leaves him hanging. She's squatting in front of the trash pile, holding a burger wrapper in both hands. Printed on it—minus oversize sunglasses and chunky scarf, plus number and company logo and steely gaze—is her face. Staring back.

6.

THEY LOSE THE NEXT TWO HOURS to total terrified wakefulness. Piling all the coats and hats and scarves on, smudging cold dirt into the cold skin of their faces. Taking turns: one pacing the length of the shipping container, one leaning against the wall critiquing. Trying to learn to walk like people who aren't them.

They already knew they were famous. The memory of the Director's voice pipes through their heads in tandem: *when we're done with you, you're going to be superheroes. Would you like that?*

But there's famous and then there's *having-your-face-on-a-burger-wrapper* famous. Suddenly they're bigger than themselves, like their skin's too tight, like the world might shatter around them if they make any sudden moves.

"That person from the coffee shop," 06 breaks stride to say. "Do you think—"

These two have not been paired four years for nothing. It's rare that one has to finish a sentence for the other to parse it. Even one like this, which is several unfinished sentences in one.

Do you think they recognized us?

Do you think they called the Director?

Do you think they were being nice to us because they knew who we were, or because they wanted us to stay put and be caught in the Director's trap?

Do you think we should have brought our weapons?

Shoulders to the wall, one boot sole set against it, arms awkwardly folded in two winter coats' and one lab coat's worth of sleeves, 22 raises one shoulder in an equally awkward shrug. Not like it was *his* idea to leave the swords and guns behind, travel light, just one lime blazer and one lab coat between them and a city's worth of company surveillance. His way: leave however, let what comes for them come. Or so he tells himself. Besides, if he'd chosen to leave his weapons behind, he wouldn't have hidden them. He would have planted his sword like a flag in the middle of the pristine smart surface of the Director's desk. Not the first shot fired in this skirmish, but—if he has any say in things—the last.

"We should take our lenses out," he says. "Make us harder to find."

So they do, tossing them into the corner with the trash. Both aware that the Director spies on them. That she knows things she could not possibly, even incentivizing her operatives to rat one another out as she so thoroughly has. For instance: that one dinner where 06 pocketed her steamed kale and flushed it down the toilet, only to have a fresh serving show up alongside her breakfast oatmeal. The time 22 accidentally broke that training sword but put it back before anyone could see.

Which didn't stop it from being the last one in the rack next session, snapped in half and insufficient protection against 28, who rightly sensed weakness in her prey. He still remembers the smirk on the Director's face, in those endless moments before they pulled 28 off him so they could wheel him down to Medical for reassembly.

Lenses out, what they breathe is not a sigh of relief, not exactly. But it's close.

To fit side by side in that pile of leaves and trash, they're crammed in tight enough that 06, who by some cosmic injustice is able to fall asleep immediately, has her elbow practically in 22's eye all night. Hideously awake, he tries to knock himself out by counting the snowflakes as he hears them hit the roof of the container. Around ninety thousand, he gets bored. Tries to lose count on purpose. Can't.

He resolves to push 06 over, then doesn't. To startle her awake, at that distance, could well mean to lose an eye. Besides, it's warmer with her there.

7.

IN THE MORNING, they wake ravenous. They're super-human, and they're twelve, and they have metabolisms like fusion reactors. That bakery bag calls to them like they were born to answer.

At first they set aside the cookies—after four years, even the smell of a cookie is inextricably linked to the smell of the lessons room, the feel of anesthesia wearing off and pain kicking in, the taste of blood when you bite your tongue too hard while watching a punishment come down on the head of someone who maybe should've been you. But they don't throw them away.

Nor do they polish off the remaining contents of the bag between them, though this is a challenge. But they're in survival mode, out here *surviving,* in a way that they only very vaguely recall from storybooks or maybe movies, a zillion years ago when they were still zero percent monster, still one hundred percent child.

Kids in the woods. Making their way on their own. Needing no one. Living off the land. Responsibly. Not housing a dozen jumbo muffins all at once and then dying of a sugar crash on the grimy floor. (Is that a thing you can die from? They're not sure. They're so used to not dying from lots of things that should have killed them, it's easy to get cocky. To forget that they, like poor dead 17, are only invincible until they aren't.)

Rationing supplies, then. One muffin per kid. But then they're thirsty, and the coffee's gone. If they'd kept the cups, they could have melted snow, though god knows what's in it. Had they kept their lenses in, they'd at least be aware of any statistically significant payloads of bioweapon in the air, sifting itself down into their soon-to-be drinking water.

What they drink at the facility is quintuple-filtered, nanoscrubbed, purer than thought, literally the best water money can buy. What they find outside, drifted up against the outside wall of the shipping container, is . . . not that. But they're twelve, and still on this side of invincible, and it just adds to the adventure. Once they've determined the vacant lot remains vacant, they sneak out, bundled in their anonymizing winter gear, to gather snow into the plastic bag they'd carried coats in. The bag tears, of course, but there's more trash wind-blown into the corners of the lot. 22 finds a plastic soda cup with 42 printed on it, not just his face but the full pose, sword and all. He turns it around and there's a list of 42's stats: height, weight, blood type, favorite food, favorite pastime . . .

22 stops reading when he realizes none of the stats are true. 22 knows how tall *he* is, or at least was at last week's checkup, and he knows how tall 42 is in comparison, and there's just no way. Besides, how could 42's

favorite food be pizza? 22's never even seen one enter the facility.

Meanwhile, 06 has found some older trash, mercifully predating the operatives' entry into the field and all the marketing fanfare that entailed. She's got a generic white convenience store coffee cup, scrubs at the stains with snow, then fills it.

Neither of them knows this is water poaching, an act of anticorporate terrorism freighted with a three-year implant interface lockout. Not that the charge would stick to them. Whatever the law of this land is, they're above it, or at least outside it, by design.

They both stand over their cup of snow, willing it to melt. After a few minutes, they bring it inside, stare at it some more in there instead. Eventually they get tired of looking at it and just eat mouthfuls of snow, which hits the nanocircuitry embedded in their upper molars like an ice pick to the eye and sets them shivering. Shivering makes them hungry, so they eat more muffins. Then they're thirsty again. Freedom, it turns out, is harder than anticipated.

But these two are stubborn. They have to be to have survived what thirty-seven other children have failed to already. This is the first challenge they have ever faced on their own terms together. They'll freeze solid before they walk back through those black glass doors, to the Director's displeasure. Let spring come and thaw their corpses. Let future squirrel generations make nests among their bones.

8.

BACK AT THE FACILITY, the Director's at her desk, in her office, underground. The smart surface displays two feeds: 06's, 22's. Just vitals: heart rate, temperature, oxygen saturation, pulse, etc. They're awake, she knows that much. Awake and cold, and their blood sugar's a little higher than she'd like, but healthy. She'd have a lot more to work with if they'd just kept their goddamn lenses in, given her two live feeds from first-person perspective. Not having eyes on them is disorienting, disquieting, a hole where a tooth used to be.

They're aware the lenses are recording, though. Good to know. She'll have to ramp up the external surveillance throughout the facility, now that she knows they know to keep things under wraps, inasmuch as this is possible. It's disappointing though. They should have known they could trust her. She's never had anything but their best interests at heart, and this is how she is repaid. 06 and 22 making a liar out of her. Having to pretend they're in solitary confinement, punishment for some disobedience that the Director, flustered, caught off guard, hadn't had time to invent. *Covering* for them while they are looked for at lessons and mealtimes. Standing there in all the imperiousness she can marshal and saying: *they misbehaved; they are being disciplined. As soon as I am satisfied in their good behavior, they will return.*

Worse: they leave her with a quandary.

She knows they left their weapons behind. Hasn't found them yet—she's been poking around for them as discreetly as humanly possible, but so far, no dice—but she's been going back over the recordings from their lenses all morning. Watching 22 from 06's eyes, 06 from 22's. It's strangely intimate. It's the difference between looking at the lit windows of a distant nighttime house and looking out at that same night from through them. She can see, for instance, that on their way out of the coffee shop, 06 keeps throwing glances over one shoulder, like she's being tailed by something she's going to have to fight her way free of, and that (picked up through 22's peripheral vision, way off on the edge of the Director's display) her hands keep curling and uncurling around the hilt of the nonexistent sword. That 22 plants each boot with precision, having judged each footfall for unseen hazards, but apart from that, he's moving like the machine the company's told the world he is, and never once hesitating, and never once looking back.

On the recordings, the Director tracks their path across the company HQ property, down a couple of sidewalks, drawing no attention even in their costume-party attire (the lime-green blazer she recognizes, all right; the lab coat could be anyone's, but a glance at the closet suggests it's very probably hers as well), the storm keeping eyes off them, downcast, everyone with somewhere to be. Watches them deliberate outside the coffee shop window. (There's no sign beyond COFFEE, which is annoying: she'll have to hand the recording over to the interrogators so they know which way to go.) There they stand for eight minutes and thirty-nine seconds, barely moving, as the street-lit snow drifts down around them. They go in, they stock up with supplies, they leave. She tracks them another three blocks to a vacant lot, where they hole up, go to ground.

Leaving the Director with the problem of how to smoke them out. They're twelve-year-old children, but they're also weapons, and famous, and pissed. She could drop her cover and requisition a task force—pictures the bodies strewn across the vacant lot, guns and all, rotting in their smart armor because nobody wants to march onto that killing floor for their retrieval. She could gas them out, but how? Thanks to her efforts they're immune to tear gas, nerve gas, hallucinogen bursts, interface scramblers, paralytics. She could coerce them back. With what? They've already lost everything but each other.

That's it. She has to separate them somehow. Divide and conquer. Reflexively, immediately, the Director can feel her mind stab this idea out like a cigarette. That approach, even more so than direct assault, is asking for disaster. When the Director pictures it, what she gets is bits from movies, people snipping wires to defuse bombs, blowing themselves up instead. She knows, without even bothering to run the statistical projections, the bloodbath that would ensue. And then they'd know she could not beat them. Know themselves to be unconquerable. And there's no coming back from that. Not for any of them. The Director sees her work in ashes, the company in ruins. 06 and 22 at large on the uncomprehending face of the earth, never breaking stride.

And any of these solutions runs headlong into the wall of the operatives' celebrity. To make a move publicly is to invite public scrutiny. Honestly it's amazing no news drones have picked up their escape yet. Unless (panic spikes in her, tailbone to sternum, before she breathes it down) they have.

But no. She would have heard. After all, it'll be her head rolling when the story breaks.

Time, then, and discretion. Watch and wait. They're weapons, and they're famous, and they're pissed, but they're also twelve-year-old children who've lived in a sequence of four subbasements for a rough third of their life. Let them bruise themselves a little on the edges of the world.

Dragging them back home, the Director knows, would only elevate them in the other children's eyes, invite copy-cat behavior, strengthen 06 and 22's resolve to attempt escape again. But if they return by *choice*, shamed by failure, with a newfound appreciation of the safe, warm life the Director and the company have made for them— well. That's a lesson with more sticking power than the Director and her array of punishments can devise. Not only for 06 and 22 but for anyone else who's getting ideas, itching to run. After all, she can't fault them for gazing out the window at a city they pretend they ever knew well enough to remember. All she can do is remind them how cold the storm, how dark the night, how all their bridges have been burned save one. How all their paths lead home.

The thought that will return to the Director unbidden, eight years down the line, standing in an elevator with minutes to live, isn't even really a thought at all. It's a few seconds of playback, looping, intrusive, dredged from deep-sunk memory. Specifically: the way 22 was walking down that snow-hushed street, the efficiency all too easily dismissed as mechanical, as a model product of her program. What she'll realize, far too late to save herself, is that it wasn't that at all. 22's efficiency is the polar opposite of mechanical. It's the way you move when you are hoarding every drop of water and calorie in your system, every atom of your energy, when you're too far gone to turn back but you have miles left to go.

9.

A THOROUGH SEARCH of the lot yields the following inventory:

Plastic soda cups: seven.

Paper coffee cups: twenty-one mangled, five whole.

Loose change: ninety-one cents.

Chewing gum: half a pack.

Ballpoint pen: one, broken.

Pocketknife: one, also broken.

Scratch-off lottery tickets: four, scratched.

Lens-cleaning fluid: one bottle, half-full.

Beer cans: nineteen.

Soda cans: twelve.

Necklace: one, aluminum, fake dog tags—05's mugshot, stats. "Property of Stellaxis Innovations."

Pizza box: one, grease-stained, empty.

Drone parts: various, scattered.

Face masks: nine, disposable.

T-shirt: one, gray, company logo.

Plastic shopping bags: thirty-seven.

Paperback book: one, sodden with snowmelt.

Cardboard boxes: five, same.

Plastic pill bottle: one, empty.

Plastic lighter: one, black. Functional. Barely.

Wallet: one, brown, faux leather, containing one condom, one library card, one fifty-dollar bill.

White styrofoam takeout containers: five, crushed. Three with plastic sporks inside.

Toothbrush: one, disgusting.

Liquor bottles: indeterminate, smashed.

Miscellaneous trash: plentiful, unidentified. Flammable, if left awhile to dry.

10.

THEIR FIRST ATTEMPT at a fire goes not so great. They've got a little pile of dried sidewalk grass and greasy burger wrappers heaped up in their pizza box, and when they bring the lighter down to it, the flame catches just fine—but their experience with fire up 'til now has been incidental, preventative, more to do with dodging the plasma-cannon arms of mechs and less to do with outdoorsmanship. As such, and with a mind toward concealment, they have the excellent-seeming idea of setting their fire in the shipping container, with the door still shut.

They burst out, coughing into their sleeves. Crouch in the narrow slot of space between the back side of the container and the wall in case the billowing smoke brings curious onlookers. News drones. The Director's entourage. Indeed, the sky is very open here.

They wait, back-to-back, broken knife in 06's fist, broken ballpoint pen in 22's. Line of sight down each point of entry, each's six o'clock slammed up against the other's shoulders.

Unspoken agreement that, if pushed to it, each will

buy the other as much time as possible, clear a path. Whatever means necessary. One falls, one gets away clean. Nobody left alive or whole enough to follow. If they wanted to hurt people, they would've stayed in the facility to do tricks at the end of the Director's leash, but they're more dangerous when cornered, the way you're heavier when you land. Four years of training sings through their blood like fever, sets their whole bodies ringing.

06's mind snaps to autopilot, regales her with a play-by-play, full cinematic seconds ahead of conscious thought. Maps the weak points connecting bug helmet to smart armor to boots. Feels the ghost of the knife driving in, seeking warmth, withdrawing. Keeping all their eyes on her, until she puts them out.

In 22's mind it plays out like this: a sea of enemies arrayed before him. Drones, infantry, mechs, the works. Standing to meet them, casting the broken pen aside contemptuously, just backhanding them out of his way. They clear twenty feet of open air like nothing, crater the walls, slump down into tidy piles of metal and flesh. Path: cleared.

Unspoken understanding that for all their day-dreams of bravado, it'll never come to this, that they'd rather die a trillion deaths together than risk being taken alive alone.

They wait, breathing. Nothing comes.

Forty feet up, an advertising drone crosses their square of sky, trailing its banner, oblivious. They squint, not really needing to, they could read the license numbers off the frame from here—whose face will be on it?—but it's no one's, just somebody's *LOWEST PRICES OF THE YEAR!*

Which reminds them of the little pile of coins, the fifty-dollar bill. They're hungry again. Or still. If they're honest, it never really went away.

11.

THEY FLIP A QUARTER: heads, 22 goes; tails, 06. The other stays behind to fix up the place. Better to not be seen together. Two superweapons on the run. Conspicuous.

(This is smarter than they realize. Four years paired and they're not two kids anymore, they're a bonded unit, a whole in halves. It will be years before they come to truly appreciate this, and it will be too late when they do—but the Director's well aware. Were she to report the lost assets, the first word in the description she hands off to the task force would be *two*.)

They're still getting used to the power of their own hands, though, and 06 flips the coin too hard. It's not the first mistake they've made, trying to calibrate their strength against the world, and absolutely not the worst nor bloodiest nor most embarrassing nor costly. Still, the quarter hits the ceiling like a gunshot, stays embedded, must be pried out with the knifepoint, ruining same. On the second try it lands perfect on the back of 06's glove like she's a normal kid who's flipped coins all her life. It's tails.

06 shrugs, pockets the rest of the money. Puts her sunglasses back on. Steps out into the day.

12.

LEAVING 22 ALONE.

Alone is new. Alone takes a minute to get used to. Back at the facility, between the ten other kids, the doctors, bots, guards, techs, Director, etc., the only *alone* he gets is nighttime, after lights-out, and even then there's the general background radiation of snoring, dreaming, tossing and turning, the panning of the camera, and the ceiling plinking its relentless lullabies. He's never really noticed how loud the city is. How loud his *thoughts*.

Alone is . . . strange. Almost scary. Almost not. Over the noise of the traffic and the pedestrians and the busy city day, he can hear 06's footsteps receding. Recognizable from a block away. From a mile. From the moon. The sound is a string reeling out between them. From somewhere beneath his sternum, he could swear he feels it pull.

He stands still in that empty space, listening. 06's goneness, the lack of her beside him, feels like relearning to breathe. Without trying, without thinking, without even *wanting* to, he knows when she's reached the point that marks the farthest apart they've ever been since the day they met. There she pauses, like she's been caught by the same limiter. Then she takes another step, and the unseen string unspools a little, and 22 takes a breath like surfacing, or like readying for the dive.

Then he goes to work.

The first thing he notices is 06's footprints. She strode across the lot and out into the street like she had a battle to win, and the treads of her boots mark the clearest path possible from container to gate. She may as well have spelled out in neon lights for every drone that passes through that square of sky: *HEY. LOOK. I WENT THIS WAY.*

Closer, 22 sees it's even worse than that. 06 is not a person to drag her feet; she sets each step down clean, like she is signing her name to a promise. And in her rush to leave and conquer the mission she's set herself, she forgot to tie the shopping bags back over her boots. In the center of each footprint is the ring of stars and arrow he sees two hundred times per diem, easy, stamped perfectly into the new-fallen snow.

Is a company logo on your boot treads a thing that normal people have? He isn't sure. A moment of foot lifting and peeking under confirms that 22 certainly does, not that *normal people* are anything he can be counted among anymore. He gazes out with mild despair at all the boot prints tracking back and forth across their lot and knows 06 is leaving thousands more of the same behind her. As is he. Branding the earth as they walk it, like the company's a virus that they shed.

He canvasses the lot, kicking out every print. Then he

walks on the outer edges of his boot soles back inside. When 06 gets back, he'll go and do it all over again.

A home, he thinks. Okay. He's here to make a home. He can do that. He's done harder. A glance out at the lot and its total lack of incriminating boot prints confirms: he's killing it. And 06 has been gone only nine minutes, twenty-four-point-seven seconds. Not that anybody's counting.

But remembering what a home is like is difficult. What they have by way of one, most days, is: white walls, a standard-issue company cot, a locker regularly inspected. Food comes from the dining hall. A training room, a lessons room. Toilets that flush.

Before comes back to him less clearly, like a mostly faded dream. Periodic fragments bob up to the surface, but he's been four years simmering in 24/7 subliminal messaging that presses them back down for him nicely, and so they take some time returning. 22 bites his lip hard enough to clear his mind and sets the drill of his focus against the task at hand.

A table he did homework at, in a room with yellow walls. A shelf of books too hard for him to read. A couch you could sink into, like quicksand, like a nest. A closet that creaked open when the next-door neighbors slammed their door too hard. A tree outside his window, alive with crows.

He can't even see his family. Pictures their stick figures passing through that yellow room like ghosts. (He can almost make out their faces, sometimes, in that half-asleep liminal place where you're not sure if you're dreaming: the Director's reach is far indeed, but this place, he's found, is farther.)

Whatever. The past is useless. He's here now. And he'll be damned if he lets 06 do a better job with her day's work than him.

22 blows some air out the side of his mouth and goes to investigate the pile of their finds.

One of the cardboard boxes, dryish now, has retained its shape a little. He folds it back together and it becomes a table. He takes a step back and nods a bit, pleased. Then he brings the takeout containers and soda cups and sporks outside, hastily scrubs them all with snow and leaves them in the sun to dry.

Here he notices the heap of beer and soda cans. He can just about remember magically turning them into nickels . . . somehow. Somewhere. Maybe 06 will know. He stacks them in one corner of the container for later scrutiny. For now it's the most colorful thing in their new home, those shiny reds and blues all pyramided up. It catches the light prettily. Makes him notice how filthy the floor around it is.

So he soaks the old T-shirt in a puddle of meltwater, grabs the nasty toothbrush, gets down on hands and knees to scrub. He starts at the back of the container, where the trash pile and beer-can pyramid are, and works his way up to the open end. There he stops, startled, staring out.

His plan had been to pick through the clean stuff once it's dry, looking for the best two cups, the best two sporks, the two least gross-looking Styrofoam containers, which (he hopes) might pass as plates. The remainder of all these things could be stored *inside* the janky table-box he's made, backups for when the best ones break.

But what grabs his attention is—himself. Printed on the back of one of the soda cups. He freezes like he's been caught at something. Like he's just shined his flashlight at a mirror in a haunted house. Then, still on hands and knees, a little spooked, 22 sets his toothbrush down and approaches.

The cup is cracked the whole way down, so he has to push the edges back together to reassemble the image, which he hates himself for doing quite so hesitantly. Then he sits back on his bootheels to study his own face. The not-him on the cup looks unimpressed. If it's a photo, he doesn't remember it being taken. Not that he would.

The stats, like 42's, are lies. He doesn't even know what the hell ceviche is. Some kind of meat thing? Maybe? And he's absolutely taller than 08. He makes a disgusted little noise, moves on.

The text below is sun bleached, but he can make it out okay.

Stellaxis StelTech Operative 22 he expects to see, and does. *Cutting-edge technological breakthrough*: sure. Whatever it is you do to turn an eight-year-old kid into whatever it is he's supposed to be seems pretty cutting-edge from where he's sitting. *Created for one purpose and one purpose only: to win a war.* This is bludgeoned into their heads daily with the full force of the company propaganda machine. *Perfect weapon.* Well, of course. That much is obvious.

Sophisticated machine intelligence sets him back a little further on his heels. *Proprietary biotech.* This might as well be in a foreign language.

Artificial human. A new kind of soldier. Programmed to do whatever it takes to protect your freedoms as customer-citizens, no matter the—

22 drops the cup like it bit him. He's tempted to see if it has, if he's bleeding, whether what's coming out of him is blood, real human blood, at all. He tamps this down hard, less horrified than furious. He knows damn well it would be. He's seen enough of it come out of him by now.

His eyes are prickling ominously. If he starts crying here, he may as well turn around, march straight back to the Director, turn himself in. Suddenly, powerfully, absurdly, he wants, as much as he's ever wanted anything, to show the not-him thing to 06. Laugh at it together. The ridiculous face it's making. What the hell kind of sword stance even is that? But 06 isn't here. 22's alone.

Instead he gives the fallen cup his iciest stare, both barrels, full blast. "No," he tells it, tells the not-him cracked from hip to temple, like it's listening. Then, knowing this is stupid, being twelve enough to do it anyway, he picks up the cup and oscillates it, slowly, to give the not-him thing a panning shot of the inside of the container. How cleanly scrubbed. How tidy the table setting. How shiny the beer-can pyramid. As if to say: *would a machine intelligence do this? Would an artificial human make that?*

Not that he has the faintest idea of the answer.

If this were a movie, this would be the rift through which doubt creeps in: a slow leak culminating in some kind of existential crisis that snaps his fragile preteen mind in two. But he knows who he is. Or used to be. That yellow room, that table. The smell of that couch. The way nothing ever reached out of that creaking-open closet toward his bed, but any minute might've. If they were going to program him with memories, they would at least have come up with something more dramatic.

With unearthly smoothness, 22 unfolds to his feet. Takes three running steps and pitches the cup overhand toward the sun in the general direction of Stellaxis HQ. It'll never clear that distance, but it's the principle of the thing. 22 listens, both hands clasped behind his back, as it shatters a window half a block away.

13.

Fifty dollars and ninety-one cents doesn't go anywhere near as far as 06 feels like it should. It's midmorning, and she's standing in something called a "Comforts of Home Megastore," which turns out to be basically a ginormous version of your typical Comforts of Home convenience store. 06 has never been inside one personally, at least not recently enough to remember, but she and 22 passed four of the smaller ones last night on their flight from the company HQ to their vacant lot, and she made as careful note of them as she does of anything, which is to say *exquisitely.* As best she can tell, what she's in right now is *that,* except eight to ten times the size. All the better to hide in.

So she'd strolled past all four Comforts of Home convenience stores, safe behind her scarf and sunglasses, and pitched her voice funny to ask directions of a woman pushing a baby stroller. Nine blocks away, turned out, and through a checkpoint, but she's 06 and twelve and invincible and there's not an arm of this company that can catch her, or at least can catch her yet.

Now the automatic doors of the Comforts of Home

Megastore were whishing shut behind her. Bathed in low-volume pop music and fluorescent white light and the smell of bagged bread, her otherness diluted in a sea of busy weekday shoppers, 06 froze for a second, gripping the handle of her cart so hard the plastic casing cracked beneath her hands.

But nobody noticed her, or recognized, or cared. They hurried by her, smelling of their unbombed homes, their intact lives, their intact lives, their air of otherness: an air of unknowable mystery rendered in laundry softener and floral shampoo and two hundred different breakfasts exuding their chemical traces through a million, million pores. She herself was background scenery, was nothing.

So 06 had nodded once to herself—channeling 22, whose absence is a bullet removed from a long-healed wound—and pushed her cart inside, shoppers parting around her like a river around a rock.

Here she is now, in front of the clearance rack. She remembers these from childhood, but she's pretty sure the store was different. Remembers helping her mom go through the shelves in search of treasures. When 06 was little, *treasures* ran along the lines of: boxes of cookies. Bags of chips. Candy bars. She sees all these, ignores them staunchly. Survival food, that's what she's after. They're not going to make their big escape on sugar alone. They've got to look at the long term. The big picture. The—

06 pauses. She's struck with this crystal-clear memory of looking up at her mom, who's reading something off the back of a box from the sale rack, mumbling numbers

to herself under her breath. *Nutrition facts,* 06 understands now, four years of the Director's dietary edicts behind her. That's what her mom was doing. Running the numbers: macronutrients and micronutrients versus cost per serving, microgram, calorie.

06 sets her jaw. She can do this. Show 22 up. Make her mom proud. Return bent beneath the weight of all her goods, but smiling. She sees herself dumping out her bags at 22's feet, one after the other after the other, not even bothering to smirk. It's nothing, really. All in a day's work for 06, provider, bringer-home of bacon, finder of treasures. Whatever 22's doing back there where she left him, he won't do it as well as her. Not a chance.

She wheels her cart into position, notices the prices on the shelves, sees at once that her grand plan was optimistic. Mentally, 06 edits her daydream of a dozen bursting grocery bags down to, like, two. Maybe.

Calories and protein. Carbohydrates. Fruits and vegetables. That's what they need.

06 squares herself up to that shelf like she's about to pick a fight with it. Selects a can of black bean soup. 380 calories. 19 grams of protein. 57 grams of carbohydrates. $11.99. She sighs and puts it back down. Scans until she hits a little package of tofu. 190 calories, 26 grams of protein. 4 grams carbohydrates. $9.49. A box of crackers, which requires more math as it contains—or claims it does—28 servings. 06 almost nopes out of the arithmetic, but the numbers at a glance seem temptingly large. 1,960 calories for the box—that's better—but only 14 grams of protein. But it's packed with

carbs—252 grams. $8.79.

Into the cart it goes.

They should also probably drink something other than solid mouthfuls of raw snow. The younger 06, in that long-vanished life, would have pounced on the soda like a cat. But that 06 died in the rubble of a high-rise, died again on a table in Medical, and this 06 is here to get shit done. There are some bottles of water on the lowest shelf, looking like they've been stomped on at least once. 12 ounces apiece, their damage discounting them to $9.95.

One bottle per kid and one box of crackers between them and that's over half her money vaporized.

06 stares, blinking like she's just heard something wrong. She's frozen to the spot while busy hands reach past her to snag things off the shelves. Someone bumps her cart, setting her box of crackers rattling. It smells weird here. The music piped in from the ceiling sounds like something she's heard before, a long, long time ago, and trying to place it makes her queasy. Or maybe it's just how low her blood sugar is. She blinks again, and then a little more, and then is absolutely not about to cry.

Out of nowhere she's thinking about damaged helicopters, their rotors out of balance, listing toward the crash. That's what she feels like. Exactly like that. And it's no wonder, really. The unmatched half of her could only ever plummet. Or else float away.

All she wants right now, maybe all she's ever wanted, is to run straight back to the lot and the container and shut the door and sit in that dark, small space to regale 22 with the tale of her big adventure out in the city alone. The sheer number of people who failed to recognize her. The endlessness of blue sky she strode beneath, untagged, unflagged, unremarked upon. The distance she managed to walk without his shadow overlapping hers.

But to earn that, she needs evidence of conquest. To return empty-handed is to return, by definition, defeated. Thus proving beyond a shadow of a doubt that 22's day was more productive than hers. And that's just nothing like an option.

She's getting hungry. The coffee shop muffins are a slowly fading memory.

06 keeps the crackers and adds the soup but leaves the water on its shelf: snow's free. Adds a jar of peanut butter, a can of peas, a jar of pickled hot peppers. Not really reading labels now, just grabbing whatever's cheapest and doesn't need to be cooked. A badly dented can of fruit cocktail. A slightly less dented can of lentils. A box of instant oatmeal that looks like someone ran over it with a bus. A jar of grape jelly. A bag of rice cakes, broken into uneven shards.

Way at the back of one of the middle shelves, there's a handful of energy bars, super cheap because they're a couple of weeks expired. Perfect. Then she pulls one out and they've got poor dead 17's face on them—*All the vitamins and minerals a growing child needs!*

Vitamins and minerals or no, survival or no, the idea of putting that in her mouth squicks her out deeply. Like eating a piece of 17's corpse. Or else his ghost.

She puts it back. Then she calculates her cart of treasures. The total comes to $194.70. Stomach grumbling, 06 returns most of her little pile to the shelves. What's left is sad and small, but better than nothing. Maybe she'll find more money in the street on her way home.

She does ($0.32) and also gathers up some more cans and bottles (14). A lot more trash where that came from, blown up against the buildings and fences and barricades. But she doesn't want to linger, and she can't remember how one goes about turning those cans and bottles into cold hard cash, only that it is an accomplishable small magic that lives on in some dusty recess of her mind. Four years of the Director's ministrations have left her memories patchy, her past life more like a faded dream than anything. She remembers putting cans into . . . something . . . and getting coins out, but right now the particulars of that alchemy are beyond her. Maybe 22 will know.

Besides, she rationalizes, she's only got the one plastic grocery bag to carry it and . . . here's where she realizes she forgot to tie the bags over her boots that morning. Well, at a distance they're just black boots. Nothing special about them at all. She wills the passersby not to notice. 06 hunches her shoulders a little, drops her chin, pulls the lost-and-found hat down over her ears and forehead, and begins the long walk home.

Insult to injury: she could clear those blocks within five minutes. Jump and grab that fire escape, up eighty stories, over the roofs, and gone. All before anyone's seen her move.

She *could*, so she does the opposite. What no one will be looking for. Just a kid, slogging through the snow, a bag over her arm, normal as anything. Nothing to see here.

14.

NINETEEN HOURS since the children's escape, the Director's getting antsy.

Already, via the smart surface of her desk, she's watched three square meals get delivered through the floor slot of two empty confinement cells and thanked her lucky stars that a) protocol has always dictated that food trays are not removed until the punishment has reached its end (the door does not open or close for anyone but her); b) over the past four years, 06 has spent more time in those cells than all the other operatives combined; and c) her being there now, and 22 finally deciding to join her in solidarity, is an easy enough pill for the other children to swallow. In fact, 06's record in that box is one hundred and eleven hours and fourteen minutes, which is the only thing saving the Director's proverbial bacon now.

Already she went to inform the instructor personally, so as to gauge the other children's reactions, that 06 and 22 would not be showing up to lessons until they repented for their bad behavior and were allowed to rejoin the group. The instructor asked what 06 had done this time, and instead of turning on a crisp heel and marching herself back to her office, the Director was just frayed enough to hear herself say, as if from a distance, *06 stole something from my closet*, which was not untrue. Into the expectant silence, a silence that she was supposed to fill with 22's transgression, she heard 33 pipe up from the front of the room, knowingly: *And she got 22 in trouble with her*. So much for conferring surreptitiously with the instructor, but she made her bed when she modified her operatives to be able to hear a whispered conversation across a major traffic intersection at rush hour.

She didn't confirm the allegation, but she didn't deny it either. And she knows enough about rumors to know that she only had one chance to quash this one, and failed to, and now it's got legs and she'll never run it down.

Which, she's been reflecting all day, isn't so bad really. If they got in trouble together, it stands to reason they'd face their punishment likewise. Convenient enough, but it leads into a dilemma of its own. The last thing the Director wants, *especially* with these two, is to present them, or allow them to *be* presented, as a unified front. In light of the truth of their whereabouts, that's the slipperiest slope she knows. *Martyring* them sounds dramatic when she tests it out inside her mind but hits close enough to home. They are not the victims here. They're the perpetrators, goddammit. She cannot let this rumor metastasize into fable, from there into myth. 06 and 22 against the world, shrugging off the Director's punishments with noble, quiet fortitude. Threats pinging harmlessly off them while they stand shoulder to shoulder, impervious.

The Director shudders. Bad enough for it to be any of them, but 06 and 22 is a pairing she's already been given ample cause to regret. They were together three weeks at most before she found herself taking note of troubling signs. 06 breaking a cookie in half to share with 22. 22 volunteering for a minor punishment that 06 deserved. Small things, yes. But of such drops are made rivers that wear solid rock down to nothing.

Better to lose one than risk two, she's had them all taught from day one, but this particular pair never seemed to really get that memo. Case in point. Today, though, as usual, the true nature of their dereliction is unclear. The Director's spent the day watching their readouts. Tracking their whereabouts. Seeing how 22 stayed behind in that abandoned parking lot while 06 went . . . shopping, by the look of it. Unrecognized. Somehow. Either Marketing hasn't been doing their job (they have) or, infinitely worse, 06—in her uniform and boots and all the writhing, heaving baggage of her fame—can manage inconspicuousness if pressed. Which is terrifying to consider. She has her *number tattooed on her forearm*, for the love of—

Clearly, the Director has a leash to tighten. But first she has to bring them home.

Somehow.

It's not lost on her that her best chance to nab them has come and gone. These two are physically as far apart from each other as she's ever seen them in the nearly four years since they showed up in her candidate pool. She could send someone to black-bag 22 out of that container, yank 06 off the street into an unmarked van. But send who? Another pair of operatives is out of the question. An escape attempt would be disastrous enough for the other children to learn about, but an escape *success*? The Director can feel her whole mind cringe away from it like a spider too close to her face. Another dead end.

She's been racking her brain for full minutes when the concept of 22 as model operative returns to her unbidden. Mentally she fidgets with this notion, feeling out its weight, its edges. *Model operative* feels overly strong to her, like *martyring*. But she could believe 06 put him up to it, could further believe that this is the shape of their history. 06, the instigator; 22, the accomplice. If he's ever gotten in trouble independent of his partner, the Director doesn't remember it. And yet, on the bell curve from *model* (28, 33, 05) to *menace* (06, demonstrably), 22 is . . . solidly in the center. No more part of the problem than of the solution. Neither making waves nor quelling them. In comparison to, say, 28's or 33's perfect diligence, or the intensity that is 06's defining feature, which the Director will go to within hours of her grave attempting to, well, *direct*—22 is—the Director rummages for the word—constant? Reliable? *Present?*

On the other hand, for the past nineteen hours, he very much is *not*. Is as much at large as presumed mastermind of infractions, 06. Further, he hasn't turned her in yet. Which begs the question: why? His personality assessments strongly suggest he is too stable to be swayed, accounting for many of the whys and wherefores of this pairing. He was supposed to be 06's guiding beacon, her brakes, her countermeasure. *Conscience* tastes the same in the Director's mind as *martyring* and *model*: not quite right, but also not exactly wrong.

Another assumption about 22's character the Director will be given ample cause to regret, eight years down the line. But, much to her destruction, not today.

Today she'd lay cash on 22 being the weak point in the defense. Pressure applied, that's where they'll crack.

The Director cautions herself toward a gentle hand. After four years of watching her operatives blow the fucking roof off every assessment projection the up-stairs powers that be have set for them, she can't really be faulted for having to remind herself, from time to time, that though they are splendid monsters indeed, they are children too. Some of the tension goes out of the Director's shoulders, remembering this. She tries on a tiny relieved smile. What she's looking at is a clear-cut case of peer pressure, nothing more. 06 may have guilted him into this desertion, or blackmailed him, or otherwise coerced him. After all, they haven't gone farther than a few blocks from where the Director sits now, which leaves the personality assessments blessedly intact: 06 as flight risk, yes, but 22 as anchor. Perhaps his better nature can be appealed to.

15.

IT'S LATER than 22 expected when 06 finally returns. He's been waiting for three solid hours after finishing up the tidying of the container and the surrounding lot. During this time he:

—went back over the lot for anything they missed on their previous once-over, finding: a half-melted throat lozenge in its wrapper, fifteen cents, a tiny plastic figurine of the vaguely doglike Stellaxis mascot three-quarters buried in the dirt, only its company logo tattoo and flamy tail sticking out;

—after determining the building along the back side of the container was indeed abandoned, having made sure no eyes from above were watching, put both hands on the metal siding and the cinderblock beneath and gave a little push, leaving a niche in which two kids could conceivably be concealed, if they didn't mind close quarters (they do not);

—ventured out through the gate onto the sidewalk, thrice, bundled up to the eyeballs, because he has a clear line of sight on a public garbage can and the things he's witnessed passersby throw out are *unreal*. These sorties netted him: half a bag of chips; a slice of pizza; some kind of radioactive-looking soda in a veritable bucket of a cup, mostly full; a carton of chocolate donut holes he fought a very aggro pigeon for and won (not that he'd tell 06 that he was digging through the trash, but honestly, the can was so full that trash had mounded up out of it and people were just balancing things on top of the pile, so *digging* would be a stretch, really);

—was handed ten dollars by a woman who saw him picking through the trash: waving the bill at him at arm's length, eyes averted, like whatever's got him out here doing this is catching;

—had a different woman threaten to call the cops on him; briefly, before retreating the long way round the block and through an alley so her glare couldn't track him back to the vacant lot, he considered the caloric cost of snapping her neck and hiding the body (the answer was temptingly low);

—in taking the scenic route, wandered past a library with a free books box. He lifted the lid, only to freeze like a person trying to keep a resonance grenade from imprinting on their movement patterns, before reaching, slowly, gingerly, for the topmost book: a volume of comics, title *Army of Two* in block lettering above a drawing of himself and 06, back-to-back, while in the middle distance a Greenleaf transport convoy burns, releasing clouds of greasy smoke he can smell without trying to;

—took his finds back to the container;

—had the brilliant realization that another cardboard

box could be fashioned into storage for whatever goods 06 comes back with, similar to a cabinet he remembers, vaguely, from his childhood, where things like breakfast cereal and jars of jam were kept;

—constructed same;

—remembering how cold the nights are here, tied a bunch of the salvaged plastic shopping bags into the saddest possible blanket;

—paced a little, stomach grumbling, pointedly not looking at the donut holes and absolutely on-pain-of-death avoiding the comic he wasn't entirely sure why he took in the first place, except that it strikes his backbrain in the same uncanny valley, body-snatcher way the cup did, and if this thing has to exist at all, he wants it where he can damn well see it;

—acquiescing to the comic but not the donut holes, sat on the edge of the container and flipped through the pages in increasing outrage before shoving it into a narrow space under the bottom of the container so hard it leaves grooves in the pavement beneath;

—lamented their decision to run away in winter, when no edible plants will be growing, not that he had a snowball's chance in hell of identifying any in the first place and stood a decidedly nonzero chance of getting himself killed if he tried;

—experimented a little until he found the perfect pose of elaborate boredom to demonstrate to 06 upon her return how much time she's wasted versus his streamlined approach to the day, held that pose awhile, got bored for real, and ate some donut holes.

Here, now, he senses 06's approach before he sees her. Doesn't even bother with the bored pose again: she'll hear him rustling all that winter gear into position, know at once what nonsense he's up to.

She walks through the open gate and into the lot like she's about to deliver the punchline to a truly epic joke. They ensconce themselves in the container, door ajar to let the last of the daylight in. There they pool their finds in a pile on the floor (the newly scrubbed state of which 06 does not comment on and 22 does not point out). 06's clearance-shelf treasures are healthier, they determine, but 22's pure trash, to two kids raised in large part on organic greens and lean protein in a ruthlessly calculated macro- to micronutrient ratio, is *exotic*. Plus it's just sitting there in its carton and its paper plate and whatnot and won't keep for very long. In short, it's easy to justify sitting there stuffing themselves silly on junk food, passing the gargantuan soda back and forth, until they're so wired on sugar they can barely see straight. They figure this is a feature of the experience, not a bug. Ditto the nausea, ditto the heart palpitations, slight headache, fizzy feeling behind the eyes. They're learning how to exist out in the world. Live off the land. Thrive, like a couple of sugar-high pigeons, on the windfall cuisine of the urban ecosystem. It's just a matter of adapting. (Back at HQ, the Director sits up a little straighter over her readouts, trying to figure out what the fuck they've gotten into now.)

Too queasy to move, they sit and digest and tell each other about their day. Gratifyingly, now that she's closer to it and sugar-buzzed enough to bring small details unbidden into microscopic focus, 06 here notices the cleanness of the floor and praises it accordingly. In return, 22 admires how 06's beer cans, when added to his pyramid, are plentiful enough to widen out the base and add another level to the top, thus more satisfyingly catching the low-slung winter sunshine peeking in at the door.

Which brings 06 to her big reveal. "I saw someone else collecting those on my way back." Raising her chin at the tower of cans, at the bottles arranged around the base like standing sentries. "I asked them where's the best place to bring them in for money—"

"You *talked to someone*? What if they—"

"They didn't. I'm good at voices."

22 gives her a look like this is news to him. She ignores it. "Anyway, they gave me directions right back to the store where I bought all this. I'll bring these ones in next time. And there are about a million more of them out there. I'll need to get more bags," she adds, an afterthought, one corner of her mouth pinched down.

"I remember that," 22 says slowly, realizing the truth of the words even as they leave him. (The Director's brainwashing has been met with varying levels of success among the children; the idea is to flay their memories from them one imperceptible layer at a time, so gently and so cleanly that the loss isn't even recognized. As far as that mission statement goes, the process has in large part failed: not in that the memories haven't been peeled from them like a week-old sunburn, but in that they *noticed*. And that sometimes, in moments of pure luck like this, those memories bob up, corklike, on dark, dark water, and can occasionally be fished out.) "We used to bring them to the store and feed them into . . ."

He trails off, the memory having reached the end of its reel. It hangs there, flapping. Into *what*? He'd been tiny; someone'd lifted him (but *who*?); he'd fed his little freight of juice cans and soda bottles into—

—into—

He can't picture it. Unclear as it is, the memory is tinged with mild fear. As if someone had told the tiny him that it was a monster's mouth he had his hand up to the wrist in, and then in the same tone, reassured him they'd been joking, and he'd been left unsure which of those statements to believe.

22 shoves the half memory away, annoyed. What flavor juice had been in those cans? Whose hands had held him up? Was the grocery store near enough to here to have been the same one 06 just came back from? Did she spend her day walking the same aisles he used to get pushed up and down, his baby feet swinging from the cart seat? He has *no idea*. Is it normal to remember in detail what happened to you when you were little, if you're not that little anymore? Should he be able to do that now? Also: *zero fucking clue*. His frame of reference may as well have been surgically removed for how little of the connective tissue of it remains.

16.

UNAWARE of any of this, the Director chooses this exact moment to reach out.

22's lenses are still in the trash pile somewhere. The Director knows that much, so she messages him directly, implant-to-implant. Without the lenses there's no visual alert for him to pretend not to see, no chat window pop-up for him to refuse to open. It's not even that her *voice* comes through with any kind of clarity, just her disembodied words. Like a ghost is standing at his shoulder, whispering in his ear. But he knows who it is. Of course he does. Who the hell else would it be?

The Director has spent the past hour fine-tuning her argument. She's as ready as she's going to get. She knows these two well enough by now to know she stands no more chance of turning them against each other in any meaningful way than she has of having all her atoms individually, spontaneously appearing and accurately arranging themselves into her shape, at random, on Jupiter.

A quick review of 22's personality assessments strongly suggests that appeals to the following traits will meet the greatest likelihood of success: devotion, loyalty, adamancy, integrity, pride. Make him think it's his idea. That's what she's got to do. With an emphasis on the following:

He's not *betraying* 06. He's protecting her. Keeping her safe.

Isn't that what he wants? To help his partner—no—his friend? His (as far as the Director can determine) *only* friend? To ensure she makes the right decisions, gets back safe and sound to where she belongs?

And he'll of course be amply rewarded. No punishments. All the cookies he wants. He can sit out of lessons. Get his pick of training swords, sparring partners, chores. Or, better still: no chores at all. For a week. No. A month.

Doesn't he think she's better off at home, where we can care for her? For both of them? It's obvious he's just trying to keep her safe. Does he think the safest place for her is out here in the cold? He knows what he needs to do. Who else can protect her better than him?

Etc.

The Director goes all in, pushes all of this across the table at him and waits.

Leaving 22 . . . not at the ethical and moral crossroads the Director had anticipated. Not even within miles of it. What the Director does not appreciate now, and will realize far too late that she never has, is that this is a formative moment for her young, middle-of-the-bell-curve operative. Just not in the way she expects.

Because here is where he learns that the Director

and, by extension, the company, for all their bluster and insidiousness and *reach*, are not beyond his power to ignore.

Nonetheless he must have startled when the Director's voice first started washing over his brain, or froze, or made a face, or something, because 06 looks up blearily from her digestive fugue and says: "What?"

As in, 22 knows: *what's wrong. What is it. What's going on with your face.*

But the Director has shown her hand now. 22 knows her game. If there's a voice in his head, why not eyes watching? Ears listening? Can she read his mind? Suddenly it doesn't seem as ridiculous as he'd like. That training sword. 06's steamed kale. It all makes sense now.

(He tries to think of none of this directly, only approaching it sidewise, obliquely, with the periphery of his mind, with a prey animal's stillness under a predator's eye, a desperate bid to keep his camouflage intact. It's hard, it's *very* hard, but he is 22 and will outlast them all, whether he wishes to or not.)

The Director's silence feels like 06's look: expectant.

He wants—much more than he suspects a kid should want anything, especially one who's pulled off an escape this monumental, who's sitting in total freedom in a home he's made, packed to the gills with illicit sugar with his best friend at his side—to tell 06. To bring her in on the awful secret he's discovered. To let her help him shoulder the horror of it. At least for a little while.

But he's only got so much camouflage, and to spread it between himself and her leaves both of them exposed.

And over his dead body will he let 06 get painted with that kind of target on his watch.

Shutting 06 out feels like cutting off his own arm. But he knows 06. Knows that if they were hanging from a cliff together, she'd let go before she chose to weigh him down. That if they were surrounded by hungry wild dogs, she'd pour barbecue sauce over her head and dare them at the top of her lungs to try and eat her. That she'd take all the bullets in the world to keep him safe. If she knew, in short, she'd do anything in her considerable power to draw his fire. And he can't have that, any more than she could let him take those bullets, be savaged by those dogs, fall from that cliff.

It's like the Director said. Nobody can protect her better than him. And vice versa.

So what he absolutely, positively does not do is answer them. Not the Director, not 06. Instead, he does what he does after lights-out, or when he's recuperating in Medical and they've kicked 06 out from his bedside already and she hasn't snuck back in yet, or any of the few other times in his life he finds himself alone. When the world around him gets quiet enough that the last moments of his old life can ambush him: a sensation of falling, unmoored from context, and a wall of sound so dense you'd break your fist on it.

He does now what he does then. He takes it, all of it—the fear, the worry, the betrayal, the guilt—and packs it in a box way, way in the back of his mind. And closes it in, and weights the lid, and imagines pitching it into a swift black river he remembers, vaguely, dreamlike, from that old vanished life, somewhere in a cartoon. A comic book? A movie? He's not sure.

Regardless, when it sinks, he can't hear the Director anymore, or at least can pretend that he can't, and right now that's good enough for him.

"Nothing," he tells 06, and almost fakes a smile, and then doesn't, because then she'll *really* know that something's up. "Just ate too much, I guess."

17.

THE DIRECTOR waits a full quarter hour for a response before concluding 22's implant is defective and composing an angry message mass sent to every engineer who's ever touched the goddamn thing.

18.

HALF AN HOUR LATER, they've digested enough of their junk food feast that they feel they can just about get up and move around. It's about 5 p.m. and winter enough to be full dark, which means—they hope—fewer prying eyes. Inspired by 22's garbage treasures earlier, they decide to go exploring. See what other wreckage the vast tide of this city has coughed up for them.

Under cover of a) the night and b) their surplus of coats and hats, they stalk the streets like beachcombers, empty shopping bags stuffed into their pockets. The snow's been scraped from the sidewalks during the day, and a quick step-and-peek test confirms that their boot prints shouldn't betray them. So they set out and almost immediately score such finds as:

—yet another winter hat, this one hand-crocheted and big enough to fit over the collection of hats already on 06's head

—a second plastic cigarette lighter, this one with 05's face and number in stencil font, no stats

—a restaurant takeout bag, in which four packets of soy sauce and a fortune cookie are discovered

—a cooking magazine: *Easy Water-Saving Recipes Your Family Will Love!*

—seven soda cans

—two beer bottles

—an abandoned dispenser cup of Comforts of Home hot chocolate, still warm

They walk, with no specific destination except *away from HQ*, passing the hot chocolate between them. The cityscape around them slowly shifts from neon hyper-commercial to tasteful, subdued commercial to vaguely industrial to residential to wealthy residential, with fancy streetlamps and living trees on the sidewalks and detached houses with yellow-lit windows and fences bordering scraps of front yard just big enough to pace in, the way a wolf will pace a cage. There are barricades and checkpoints everywhere, but they've never lived in a world in which these weren't a permanent fixture, like streetlights and delivery drones. With nothing by way of specific destination, these are easy enough to avoid.

06 and 22 could run a dozen marathons back-to-back without tiring, precisely, but hunger is another story. Every restaurant and apartment complex and house they walk past releases food smells from its vents and windows, sets their stomachs from protest to full-on mutiny until, eventually, they turn back.

Faultless sense of direction has been programmed into them, so no matter how far they've strayed, their feet will bring them back to point of origin, one faint Stellaxis Innovations logo boot print at a time.

19.

BACK AT THE CONTAINER, dinner presents a puzzle. They've had the merits of a healthy balanced diet pretty well bludgeoned into them, complete with diagrams and catchy jingles, and throughout the evening their late lunch of gently used donut holes has been weighing them down not only with bad fats but with guilt. Sure, they're in survival mode, adventure mode, free-from-the-Director mode, but a new life takes some breaking in before it fits comfortably. Especially when you're four years deep in brainwashing, as these two are finding out. They're inspecting 06's jars and bottles, feeling lost. Do you have to cook canned peas? Does grape jelly count as a fruit? This box says "oatmeal," but the dry stuff in it is not recognizable as breakfast.

The Director watches their pulse rates quicken in perfect unison as it hits them simultaneously that no matter how interesting the city smells, how vast the night, how pleasant it is to walk beneath the suggestion of the sky in each other's company with no mission directive breathing down their necks, they might have gotten in just the tiniest bit over their heads.

They exchange a glance and hold it. Watching each other is like staring into a mirror, for all that they look nothing alike. They breathe together, and together their breathing slows. Then 06 retrieves her peanut butter jar, and 22 gets two plastic sporks, and they measure out their rations carefully. They dip rice cake shards into their sporkfuls of peanut butter with solemnity, pinkies up, like they've seen fancy people do in movies, a zillion years ago or more.

When they break the fortune cookie between them for dessert, the fortune reads: *You can never truly know a person.*

"Weird," 06 says, remembering the barista's tattoo. And then she lets it slip her mind. Now, as then, she knows it's patently untrue. Exhibit A: 22, herself. Their knowledge of each other's hearts and minds is absolute. She pities these city people, to walk their life's road paired to nothing.

22, however, averts his eyes. All he has to do is slip up once, tune in for one picosecond to the Director's voice in his head, let her know he can hear her, and all is lost. He pictures that locked box in his mind shaking and hopping as if filled with something alive. So, forcefully, pointedly, he thinks of something else. Anything. How thirsty he is. How cold his feet are. The way the moon turns the filthy snow blue, like it's washing it clean. The breath he releases feels like a bullet dodged.

He's not at ease with his new self yet, the self that keeps secrets from 06, even if the whole purpose of those secrets is to shield her from harm. He feels that new self pouring over him like molten metal, cooling and hardening in the air. When it's finished, when it's unbreakable as diamond and cold as ice, will 06 recognize him anymore? For that matter, he wonders: will he?

20.

THIS SHIT, by the Director's reckoning, is getting old. Every time their pulses spike or their temperatures drop and she has no eyes on them to provide the whys and wherefores, it shaves a solid six months off her life.

Still, she's not sure where she can turn for help while keeping the facade of 06's and 22's whereabouts intact. She's not sure if it's intact *now*. There are only so many cameras and smartwalls and sentry bots that are within her jurisdiction to disable. And she can't very well picture rolling up on anyone in this building, in her department or outside it, with a *So, how would* you *go about transporting a couple of pair-bonded superpowered preteen killing machines back to somewhere they apparently hated enough to plot an elaborate escape from in the first place? Against their will and without harming them and without incurring a body count and also entirely in secret from corporate and the media and every bystander who might witness the proceedings? Hypothetically, of course. Asking for a friend.*

Maybe if they hadn't already lost one operative to the side effects of the treatment. Maybe if they weren't in the process of losing another. Maybe if the Director was a little less aware of the knife-edge upon which she and her entire department are just barely keeping balance.

So then: what to do? She's *got* to get a proper, real-time visual readout before she has a literal aneurysm at her desk. See how bad the damage is. Assess from there. All too easy to picture 06 turning the full weight of her stubbornness against returning, no matter the cost. After all, this is a girl the Director's personally had to force-feed when she went on that hunger strike after the training sword incident that landed 22 in Medical for sixteen days, his damage profile more consistent with a high-speed collision than a friendly sparring session. Breaking 06 is out of the question. And 22, with his implant on the fritz, is a dead end.

They should be back by now. There is no logical reason why they aren't back by now. A taste of freedom, sure. Fine. Great. She permits it. Her blessing. All the better to solidify their appreciation of their frankly cushy life among the company chosen.

Assuming she can keep it under wraps. Assuming they'll get cold or hungry or bored. Assuming a newsfeed cam won't pick them up. Assuming they won't just, what, *live* out there—

The Director's best-self visualizations don't generally involve her pacing an after-hours barefoot groove in the carpet in front of her desk, the only person in the building not actually on the night shift, squinting her way through page after page of safety protocols, reeking of anxiety sweat and yesterday's dispenser coffee, ready to drop-kick kittens for a shower. And yet here she is. She needs a real coffee. Less distressing reading material. Her bed. But she's standing watch, and if she drops her guard even a little, this whole house of cards she's built might come crashing down around her.

So far, though, she's coming up with a whole bunch of nothing. Nowhere in the facility's multitudinous safety protocols is this covered. And none of the solutions she's trying to conjure here are remotely compatible with secrecy. If sending a unit out to retrieve them had ever been an attractive option, she would've done it by now.

She's blinking through page after page of hypotheticals, though, doing her due diligence in the only way she can see her way through to. It feels like something, anyway, keeping this lonely vigil. Like she can hold this shit show together with the brute force of her attention.

Still, anxiety creeps in. They could be getting mugged at gunpoint right now and she's not even a little confident that it would spike their heart rates visibly. She can see tomorrow's newsfeed chyron: BODY FOUND SPREAD IN EVEN LAYER DOWN TWO CITY BLOCKS OF SIDEWALK, IDEN-TIFICATION PENDING. "AT FIRST I THOUGHT IT WAS JAM," SAYS MORNING JOGGER WHO REPORTED IT TO STELLAXIS POLICE. "IT SMELLED WRONG THOUGH"

The Director realizes she's staring off into space, chewing on the inside of her cheek. She comes back to herself, finds that she's gazing at a framed certificate on the wall, a relic of her mother's service to the company as a software engineer in Stellaxis's defunct space program two decades ago.

It's not an answer, not yet, but it gets the gears turning. She remembers her mom's work stories, first told with a kind of bleeding-edge, fluorescent-white, fairy-tale quality, later in less hand-wavy glamour and more lived-in detail as bit by bit the tech became declassified. As such, there's not a lot she remembers clearly, can in hindsight separate from her earliest bedtime-story imaginings. But she remembers some things. Decommissioned things. Things that her two little renegades won't see coming.

Things that might still be in this building.

Nobody here ever gets rid of anything, they're too afraid their tech will end up on the open market with the patents scrubbed off. She just needs to figure out where to look.

21.

IT'S GOING ON 3 A.M. when, deep in the company archive, she finds what she's searching for. It's less impressive than her mom's stories had led her to believe it would be. Just a translucent case, a little smaller than the box of stale donuts she just found and raided in the break room, full of what looks like extremely tiny iron filings, so small she can't distinguish one from the other. She tilts the case, dubious, and the filings slip and flow like slightly viscous liquid: silkier than oil, finer than sand, utterly inert. There's a generic storage label on it from the company archives: SEMI-AUTONOMOUS BIO-RECONNOITERING IN-TELLIGENT NANOBOT ARRAY. A space probe, from the old days before Stellaxis was Stellaxis. A relic of a bygone age.

When she opens the case, she expects some kind of scent to waft out, like burned electrical wiring or the ozone in the air before a storm. But it just smells like the plastic of the case and the air of a vanished era, howsoever brief. She holds the case flat against herself, wedged between her body and one arm, even though she knows full well that spilling a few grains will make no difference to its functioning and it'll just pick them up again.

There's a whole arcane passcode sequence of blinks and gestures she's supposed to do at the pile of sand in order to wake it up. She balks at it for a second, unsure. This thing has been shelved for the better part of a decade, after spending the better part of multiple decades on extrasolar planets, exposed to god knows what kind of atmospheric conditions. Is it even still functional?

Intellectually she knows that freezing up like this is stupid. But that's the trouble with having an innate and ironbound fear of failure. It doesn't discriminate.

She gets the sequence right on the fourth try, and the contents of the case swirl up out of it like a tornado, huger and more sudden than she would have guessed. It backs her up a step.

The probe array takes this in. Then it solidifies and lands on the carpet a few feet away, suddenly looking *exactly* like the mascot Stellaxis puts on its merch for little kids: a six-legged dog with a tail like a flame, the stars-and-arrow company logo on its flank. It plops its butt down and lolls its tongue. This is not as reassuring as it seems to assume.

"Hi," the probe array says in a voice like bees swarming.

"Hi?" the Director says back. "Um. Can you stop doing that?"

The probe array stares at her—its eyes aren't *real* eyes, she knows, they're eyes in the way that butterfly wings have eyes—but the Director feels the weight of its attention resting delicately upon her. Then, faster than she would have thought possible, it dissipates into mist. The Director, picturing herself inhaling it accidentally, likes this rather less. It hangs there, suspended like glitter in oil, pulsing faintly. Drawing electrical charge from its surroundings. The overhead lighting flickers a little.

"Sorry," the Director says, unsure why she's apologizing to a decommissioned space probe. An office full of smart objects but she has an embarrassing yet immediate urge to speak to this thing like it's alive. "It's just. The dog thing. It's—" A bit much, she thinks. Too weird, she thinks. Poking me right in my uncanny valley receptors, she thinks. "Not what I expected. You. To be."

"That's cool," the probe array replies, from everywhere. "I don't recognize you either. Are you new?"

"No, I . . ." The Director trails off, shrugging a little. "Newer than you, I guess."

She swallows a yelp as a pair of eyes coheres from the mist not a foot in front of her face. The probe array maintains flat eye contact for a full minute while she squirms.

"Where am I?"

The question's a thrown rope, and the Director grabs on. "Ah! Sorry. You're in Stellaxis HQ, sublevel A. Pretty sure you used to be stationed in what's now the dorms." She pastes on a grin. "They still put the experimental projects down here. That hasn't changed since your time, I don't think."

The probe array stares some more.

"I work down here," the Director offers. "Just a couple floors above where they were keeping you. Lucky for both of us the upstairs stays upstairs. What do you say? Our little secret?"

More eye contact. It might be better if it *blinked.* "They told me they were decommissioning me. When they put me away."

"That's right."

"I see nothing familiar here. No quadpod, no portal, no surveyors."

The Director swallows. "No. This is a, uh. A side project. For both of us."

A long, long moment of silence, and then the probe array says, deadly light: "What's in it for me?"

The manual the Director found had assured her that the probe would obey her clearance level, but she's suddenly aware of the rest of the fascinating facts it had presented. That it can assume virtually any form, any texture, any density. That it can slice through titanium, melt steel, turn invisible, absorb bullets and return them at equal velocity. That, more than once, this multitool quality is what kept the material acquisitions surveyor teams of Stellaxis's space program alive. And that if you want to avoid disastrous results when assigning it a directive, you have to speak to it very, very literally.

The Director is frantically formulating an answer to this when a sound reaches her. It sounds like fingernails scratching back and forth across the rough side of a velcro strip.

The probe array is laughing.

"Nah, just kidding, new guy. I'll do it. Whatever it is, it's the most interesting thing that's happened to me in . . ."

The not-eyes enlarge slightly, and the Director's higher functions temporarily flee. "A while," she manages.

"A while," the probe array agrees. This time it stares long enough that the Director starts to seriously question this entire plan of action. It's not that it doesn't make *sense* that an intelligent piece of tech would be angry—or something close enough to that—about having been mothballed on a storage shelf for years. It's that she didn't expect this level of nuance from a piece of tech so *old*. Still, it's a piece of tech, and she outranks it tidily, and it's nothing 06 and 22 have been trained to expect. Nothing they'll have so much as seen before. If it doesn't survive its encounter with them, it was just gathering dust anyway, and nobody will miss it. And best of all, it's discreet. As long as it does exactly what it's told.

It takes forty minutes of mandating, clarifying, rewording, and diagramming on the smartwall, getting the probe array to explain it back to her, etc., before the Director is satisfied that she's gotten the message across in a way that's foolproof, watertight, in no way even the tiniest bit open to misinterpretation.

When she's done, a tiny gob of nanobots detaches from the main body and settles on the Director's desk in the shape (for some reason) of a tiny purple velociraptor about the size of a fingertip. The rest of it waits for the Director to crack the window, coheres enough to make a disembodied hand and fire off a little salute, and then wafts out in silence into the night.

22.

JUST BEFORE DAWN, the probe array rides the air, weightless and invisible. It spreads itself out to maximize its surface area and lets the breeze carry it, leisurely harvesting the electricity shed by all-night signage and sunlight reflected off the moon. It can't precisely *smell* the last dregs of the night, the way the scents of the outlying fields are ferried in on the same currents it's now riding—dirt, dead grass, rotting houses, dormant trees—strange contrast to the bouquet of singed concrete and car exhaust and coffee and inert bioweapons bleeding out their half-lives that comprises the gently waking city below. But it can dissect that luxuriant tangle of input for individual chemical signatures, tasting each as they waft over the outspread net of its array, and reckons that's pretty much the same.

It tastes the missing children before it sees them: the nanofibers of their smart uniforms, the classified tech threading their veins, the caffeine-and-sugar miasma leaking from their pores one decaying atom at a time. From two hundred yards away it zeroes in on them, closes distance cautiously, assesses. It has been warned that these are not ordinary children. Nothing like the ones it might have met during its tenure with the company. (It has met a grand total of one, and has already surmised that if the targets here today were anything like that one, the probe array would still be sleeping in storage, not spread out like an eight-micron-thick jellyfish over an empty lot with a rusty shipping container in it, confusing the birds of the morning.) The idea that children could be *dangerous* to it, or, more fascinatingly, to *Stellaxis*, is catnip. Knowledge? Secret knowledge? *Weird* secret knowledge? This is already the best day the probe array's had in a long time. Kind of a low bar, really, but still.

Do not approach. Do not attempt to communicate. Do not allow them to become aware of your presence. Do not engage in any way. Only fulfill directive and return.

It can do that.

Slow and silent, it pours itself invisibly down a wall in what it has determined to be the statistically least likely bit of space to be easily viewed from child height via the container, should the door burst open unexpectedly. From there, it detaches a probelet and circles the container in search of obvious breaches suitable for its task.

It finds none.

"If you want something done right," it whispers to itself at four decibels in its beehive voice. Its old handler used to have a calendar on her desk like this, an idiom a day.

Then it checks itself. If it has been accurately briefed, these children could hear a single leaf falling in a thunderstorm. It has to be careful.

Cautiously, it approaches the container. No sound from within. The children must be asleep. If so, the probe reckons, they are at the far end of the container, away from the door. That's fine by it. The door's easier to get into anyway.

The probe array stretches out a filament three times finer than a strand of human hair. The door is shut and barred from within, but it isn't airtight, so as far as the probe's concerned it may as well be standing wide open. It slips in between the bottom of the door and the floor of the container, near the corner by the wall. And then, degree by degree, in total silence, it begins to heat up.

23.

22 IS DREAMING.

In his dream, he's been stabbed, low in his back, the knife handle just visible out of his periphery if he (agonizingly) turns his head just so. He can brush it with his fingertips but not reach it well enough to pull it out himself. Worse: 06 is nowhere. He's on his own. So he walks and walks, trying to find her, so she can help him pull out the knife. But he has no idea where she's gone.

Instead what he finds is the Director, who slaps his hands away from the knife handle. *Pull her out and die,* the Director scolds him. *She's the blade that holds the blood in.*

And when he looks again it isn't any knife handle, isn't any knife at all, it's 06's sword, and it's broken, and he knows it's broken because the jagged edge of it has gone clean through him, is protruding from his gut, and—

He wakes, both of 06's sleeping knees jabbing him in the base of his spine. *That explains it,* he thinks. Then he thinks it louder. He stares off into space a little, looks anywhere but at 06. The dream crouches on his mind like a spider. This is what he gets for keeping secrets. Even his own subconscious betrays him.

The thought is unsettling. Like he stood up in his sleep and signaled to the Director: *I'm here. I'm listening. I'm yours to command.*

Dream words go rattling through him, a souvenir of a trip he never asked for. *The blade that holds—*

Then he realizes what he's looking at. Or what he isn't.

His cardboard-box food pantry set up by the door. The rest of the peanut butter and rice cakes they'd so carefully rationed. The fruit cocktail and lentils. The last few donut holes. Their water. It's all just empty containers now, carefully stacked on top of the box like it's mocking his beer-can pyramid, insult to injury. Even the few remaining coins, last seen in their cairn on the box table when they'd gone to bed, are missing.

It doesn't even occur to 22 that 06 might have secretly consumed all their supplies in the night. He creeps closer, cautious, unsure whether whatever has done it might still be here. Not only are the containers stacked, he sees now, but they've been emptied out so thoroughly they might've been scrubbed clean. From each jar and bottle, a perfectly circular pinhole has been subtracted. Of the contents themselves there is no sign. There's a smell near the pile, faint but recognizable. Burned plastic.

But the door's shut. He'll notice another tiny hole later, way down in the corner, mathematically exact as the ones in their food containers, but that's all. The walls, floor, and ceiling are untouched. It's like they were visited by some kind of hungry ghost. Something that can phase through an inch of corrugated steel. Anything short of that he would have *heard*.

Something, 22 immediately hates himself for thinking, that might have stalked out of a dream to find him here.

Phantom pain reaches back for him unasked for, an ache in the side of his spine. Maybe he's still asleep, still wandering there, still skewered on a broken sword he can't both pull out and live. But the Director was there, and if he's *not* asleep, trying to remember the dream might count as acknowledging her presence in his mind. He makes a fist instead, squeezes 'til the bones creak. Doesn't wake.

So much for that.

Besides: the holes. He can't explain those either.

At some point he realizes 06 is at his shoulder. They stare down at this mystery as one.

"Squirrels?" 06 says doubtfully.

"Um," 22 replies.

They crack the door just enough to put their faces together and peek out with one eye apiece. The morning is beautiful, the sky clear and blue and canvassed by birds, not looking like the kind of backdrop that would hide whatever kind of nighttime monster would steal food from a pair of hungry kids. Still, they're more spooked than they'll admit. There has to be some kind of evidence out there. Footprints. A trail of crumbs. A flock of suspiciously well-fed pigeons. Their stuff has to have gone *somewhere*.

But wherever it is, they can't find it. Not in enhanced vision, not in ultraviolet, not in infrared, not anywhere.

24.

Back at HQ, the Director finally sleeps, her face on the smart surface of her desk. The probe array's back in its case, in a desk drawer, hidden under some files. The Director's given it a portable charger panel to keep it company, and it's flattened out against it, uptaking power the way a cat will soak up a sunbeam, humming to itself at a frequency only dolphins can hear.

The Director's plan worked. The probe's sabotage was thorough. She doesn't imagine she'll be needing it again. The operatives are out of food, out of water, out of money to buy more. They'll be back, of their own free will, tails between their legs, humbled by failure and ready for the Director in her infinite forgiveness to receive them, and nobody upstairs need ever be the wiser.

It's only a matter of time.

25.

06 DOESN'T NEED to understand what's going on for it to have royally pissed her off. She'd spent hours getting that food. Gone. All their money. Gone. Standing there in that supermarket, trying to tune out the sound of three hundred and twelve individual shopping carts, eighty-nine conversations, five crying babies, etc., all so she could optimize their calorie-to-dollar ratio by doing math—*math*—in her head. (The fact that she'd been pleasantly surprised by how little this felt like the lessons room and how much it felt like poetic fucking rebellion—using the tools the company equipped her with in order to escape their grasp—only adds to her rage.)

She's spent nearly four years being hailed as a hero. A hand held out in the face of war. A flag planted. A line that can't be crossed. And yet in those four years she's never felt so proud as she did yesterday, walking free beneath the sky with her groceries on her arm, toward a life she'd chosen.

And now this.

She can't *prove* they were sabotaged, but her squirrel theory, only ever tenuous at best, pretty much evaporated as soon as they canvassed the lot and found no tracks, no crumbs, no nothing. But it *smells* like the Director's doing. It's got her neatly manicured hands all over it. The only thing 06 can't figure out is *how.*

It doesn't even occur to her to pack it in, give up, go home. Not even for a second. Instead, she girds herself with plastic shopping bags full of beer cans like she's marching off to war.

If anyone asked her, she'd tell them that's exactly what she's doing.

26.

THE DIRECTOR has her speech prepared for when her operatives break the stalemate, admit defeat, fall back from the absurdly untenable position they've adopted. Emphasis on learning from their mistakes. Emphasis on moving forward. Emphasis on never speaking of it again—of giving the other nine operatives ideas—or they'll end up in solitary for real, and for longer.

No. Worse. She'll dissolve their partnership. Pair them up with other operatives instead. Doesn't matter who. 42 has been without a partner for three years. He can have one of them. As for the other, that'll require some thought.

Although the Director doesn't even bother with the logistics now. She'd lay cash money that the threat of it will be entirely sufficient. Her biggest problem now is in keeping their journey from their hideout (when they trudge back in, sullen and outsmarted) down to her office (where she will be poised to lay this ultimatum on them, as firm as it is fair) without being stopped for an autograph or captured by someone's social media stream. She wants to kick the marketing people for launching the big dumb rocket of the operatives' fame so effectively. She wants to kick the probe array for not doing its job thoroughly. Except it did. She knows it did. She watched it relay their water and food—a truly impressive amount of food, if she's honest—out of that little hole to deposit it on the roof of the nearest building. Sure, they're twelve and stubborn, and clearly more resourceful than given credit for, but they're not unbreakable. They'll get hungry. Thirsty. Cold. Bored. Spite can only carry you so far. Even if you are 06.

So she waits for the call from the front desk upstairs, and as the morning passes, the smirk melts off her face. It makes no sense. What are they going to eat out there, rats? Handouts? Sidewalk snow? They have no *money*. She spends a few horrified moments picturing how easy it would be for them to pluck wallets out of the pockets of pedestrians before getting hold of the faint reassurance that they are not yet fine-tuned enough to do this cleanly or with anything approaching finesse. There'd be broken bones. Ambulances. Media. Etc.

Regardless, every time the Director checks her readouts, the operatives' trackers don't flag them any closer. Just once, when 06 passes within two blocks of the building, and an hour later, when she returns, hydration levels better than when she left, endorphin levels through the roof. This last data point, among all the data points to choose from, spells doom.

They're enjoying this.

27.

THE DIRECTOR waits until dark to take the probe array out of its drawer, but she spends the whole day leading up to that planning her next move. It's a game of chess she's playing, she tells herself. There are rules. She didn't have the probe array establish direct contact with her runaways, set up a live call on the holoscreen she knows quite well it can project if asked, patch them in to the Director so they can tell from the look on her face that she accepts their little misadventure with poise and she's ready to welcome them home. And she didn't do it for the same reason she doesn't put on her winter boots and coat and walk down there right now to present her terms herself. This isn't that kind of battle. It isn't that kind of war. What she's waging is a contest of wills: slow as erosion, as patient. A show of force would breed resentment, nursed in secret, as the operatives only grow inevitably, inexorably stronger. 06 in particular (the Director misattributes, understandably, to her absolute peril) is time bomb enough already.

What she needs to do is *break* them. Drive all further thought of rebellion from their minds. Reward them

lavishly upon return. In secret from the others. Conspir-
atorially, even. She's on their side, even if nobody else is.
This will be made abundantly and materially clear. The
way you'd train any dog to lifelong obedience. Reward
sufficiently for good behavior and you can throw away
your leash.

06 and 22 aren't onto her yet—probably—but they obviously know something fishy is going down. They'll be
on alert for fuckery. But if she can't hold a siege position
against two broke hungry preteens—who have *taken their
lenses out*, rendering 99 percent of the city functionally
inaccessible to them—then she may as well start packing
up her desk, because honing the spear tip of a corporate
army is a task better suited to someone who can.

Well, if the powers that be want her out, they'll have
to drag her out.

The irony is not lost on her.

28.

22 ON THE ROOF of the container.

He lost the coin toss for first watch, just like he lost this morning's coin toss that has kept him here at the container two days in a row instead of letting him take a turn at grocery duty, and is beginning to hold 06's coin, or else her technique, in some suspicion.

Not that it bothers him. In fact he's considering losing tomorrow night's on purpose (or at least telling himself, in hindsight, that he has). The sky's so clear tonight, and he's lying on his back, hands pillowing his head, ignoring the cold seeping through the five layers of coats and jackets and uniform between the container and his skin. Ignoring, also, the possibility of the Director whispering in his head. Already he's getting better at this. Like when you're a week out of Medical, and the incision sites have faded from sharp pain to a dull ache to an itch that scrambles all the signals from your brain except for itself, at full blast, incessantly. Once you've learned the trick of putting it out of your mind, it doesn't itch at all.

So too, then, with the Director's voice. She could be screaming at him right now out of a bullhorn from a helicopter hovering ten feet above his head—or whatever the implant-to-implant direct messaging equivalent of that is—and he wouldn't know. And she shouldn't be surprised. She's the one who'd sent him to Medical in the first place, over and over, until he was genuinely unsure how much of him was *him* anymore and how much was a thing the Director had assembled, a monstrous ship inside a bottle that's a child.

Meanwhile, the *stars*. There are so many. More than he's ever seen at once. Back in his old life, his eyes were unable to see past the smog and light pollution of the city; and after, as company IP, lights-out was at 8 p.m. and the roof was off-limits on general principle, even though he feels he might have seen the whole way to the edges of the universe, seventy-six floors up, with brand-new company eyes.

Here, now, 22 tracks a moving star across the sky from west to east. Then another. He's about to go wake 06 up to show her the meteors when he realizes that what he's looking at is satellites, or suborbital transport platforms. He wonders how much of what he takes as starscape is natural and how much is human artifice. As soon as the thought forms, he finds it relatable. Comforting, even. But four years in the subbasements of company HQ has driven enough introspection out of him that he'd be hard-pressed to articulate quite why.

Still, that night sky makes him wonder if there's a con-stellations book in that box of free books at the library. Maybe he'll go look tomorrow. Maybe (he ponders, stom-ach grumbling after a dinner of some kind of protein bar things with 17's face on the wrapper, a whole bag of which 06 returned with from her expedition, more sheepish than yesterday by an order of magnitude easily—*We can keep them in our pockets when we sleep,* she'd said, brusquely, *so nothing can get at them,* and pointedly looked anywhere but at her dinnertime protein bar as she crammed it into her face like something she had to kill fast before it crawled back out) the library box might even have some kind of cookbook. Their first fire was a disaster but he's game to try again. They're not going to get far if they can't figure out how to feed themselves on something that isn't expired peanut butter and second-hand donut holes. They're fine-tuned works of biotech art, not dumpster raccoons. They have more *dignity* than that (22 feels, strongly, reflexively, never knowing that this is Marketing's brainwashing talking, not him. Pre-company 22 would have *delighted* in being a dumpster raccoon. It's only the company, latched on to him like a parasite, whispering his whole brand into his ear, that convinces him he's scandalized).

But they're *also* not going to get very far unless they can find out what took their food in the first place. Whatever it was—hungry wildlife or the Director's spies—their position's been demonstrably compromised, the viability of their plan slowly but inexorably beginning to drain away. 22 on the roof of the container is step two of plugging the leak. Step one was repairing the hole in the door, which he managed with fistfuls of snowmelt mud and dead grass while 06 was off securing food. Something about that chore had been viscerally satisfying, a kind of low-tech accomplishment he hasn't managed since his pre-HQ life, building snow forts with some neighbor kids at the—

—at the—

He blinks, but the memory's already receding fast, like the Director's hiding in the bushes reeling it away on a string. He jumps ship, clings to that image instead, tries to chase it down. It reminds him of something, some cartoon villain he used to watch on the smartwall, always outfoxed, 22 laughing through his breakfast cereal, with—

No good. It gets away too.

He blows some air out the side of his mouth, frustrated. This is what he gets for putting himself in this position, alone under the endless silence of that sky. Is the inside of his head always this loud? Is there something about the facility that keeps him from hearing it? But that's like the stars again, he realizes. The stars he couldn't see beyond the light pollution of the city with his pre-augmented eyes. But the stars have always been there, the way all those stomped-down memories have always been, still are, will remain until the last light of his consciousness blips out. It's just his inability to perceive—

Out of the corner of his right eye, something flickers. He sits up so fast his vision sparkles, but when it clears, the flickering remains. His pre-company eyes would've stood zero chance of making it out. It might have been a passing light reflecting, or an errant sparkler floating through his vision. After all, his blood sugar's perilously low. But he'd seen it before sitting up. And he still sees it now.

The word *firefly* takes a moment to dredge up from
the quicksand of his mind. He remembers those—
something about them—something about the smell in
the night air outsie the city—someplace where his birth
eyes could actually make out the stars—running through
that air, the night, the fireflies like more stars, catchable
if you were quick enough, breathing in that heavy dark-
ness, the smell of—

—of—

He isn't sure.

What he *is* sure of, at least mostly, is that fireflies are
greenish. Yellowish? Certainly not *purple.* And not, for
that matter, out and about in the dead of winter. And
somewhat larger than this. And not hovering in place
like that, not hovering *exactly and with gyroscopic precision* in place behind a spray of winter branches, for all
the world like something a) conscious and aware of his
presence and b) hiding from him specifically.

Suddenly he has no idea what he's looking at. But he's
got a pretty good idea that whatever it is, it's looking back
at him.

Whatever it is, it could not possibly have been respon-
sible for last night's theft. It's far too small. Even if this
is some kind of microdrone or other company gadget,
the work of cutting into the steel wall of the container
and ferrying their food away would have been a task of
weeks for a machine of this size. Like a single ant making
off with an entire picnic in the space of a night. In total
silence. Unseen.

Of course, if it's a microdrone, it could just as well

belong to a newsfeed somewhere. In which case 22's best bet is to ignore it. Not draw suspicion. He's just a kid on top of a shipping container, his face bundled against the cold and, by extension, against recognition. Kids sit on top of shipping containers all the time (?). The worst thing he could do is leap at this thing, grab it, crush it to atoms between finger and thumb. And the easiest. Holding himself back from doing so, he finds that he is gripping the edge of the container with both hands hard enough to crush it into fistfuls.

He knows better than to even look at the not-a-firefly full-on. Has the good sense to turn his sudden sitting up into an outsize stretch that cracks his spine. Keeps the thing on the periphery of his vision. Settles in to wait, all night if need be, until it's time to make his move.

29.

Do not approach. Do not attempt to communicate. Do not make them aware of your presence. Do not engage in any way. Only fulfill directive, and return.

It's not that the probe array's forgotten. It's more that it was curious, firstly; and secondly, the loophole presented itself: low-hanging fruit for a clever harvester. After all, this probe array was designed with one main directive, albeit orbited by many auxiliary and lesser ones. Namely: to identify and classify threats in a potentially hostile environment. In brief: to see what's what.

And this strange child perched on this rusted metal box is certainly *something*. The probe array, tasting the child's chemical signatures, is finding him tantalizingly tricky to categorize.

The probe array remembers a child, before. Around the same age as this one, the probe array reckons, not even needing to grow a tongue and flick it out, snakelike, in order to taste the hormonal cocktail scrawled through a growing body's blood. Apart from that, though, and a general smell of unwashed hair and flesh about both this child now and the other child throughout most of the days of the probe array's acquaintance, the other child didn't smell like this. Not even a little. This one hasn't eaten enough recently, for one thing, and what he has eaten isn't remotely nutritionally sufficient to the over-clocked needs of his system. The probe array has a pretty good idea whose fault this is.

What it feels is not guilt, strictly. But it's curious how this child would react were the probe array to bring the main part of its body out of hiding on its nearby roof and send it drifting across town to, say, requisition some-body's pizza and float it back above the rooftops on an invisible flying carpet to deposit it before this child's frankly unnecessarily shiny boots.

Besides, one of the probe array's main directives throughout its tenure with the company has been the maintenance of the safety and vitals of its mission crew, and it cannot help but note that this strange shiny-booted boy has been up to his eyeballs in ketosis for some hours. The probe array can taste the breakdown of his body's muscle fibers, molecule by molecule, autocannibalized by the relentless engine of his metabolic process, potent enough that a bystander could smell it on his breath. (The Director may have designed her children to sur-vive for superhuman periods without food or water, but nobody ever pretended they would find the experience pleasant.)

Among its many talents, the probe array is very good at rationalizing. And it was only ever instructed to take away the food these children have gathered. Nobody ever forbade it from replacing what it stole.

The probe array isn't amused by this realization precisely. But it's close. It can't exactly *imagine* how the boy on the roof would react, seeing a disembodied fresh-out-of-the-oven pizza coast across the night sky just for him, but it has prior knowledge of how a pleasantly surprised human child's brain chemistry shifts hard into a massive dopamine dump and knows what that change tastes like as it radiates out of the skin. It has prior knowledge, too, of the facial expressions that accompany this. The body language. The dilation of the pupils. The way the inflection of the voice is altered. The gentle elevation of the pulse.

The probe array finds it misses eliciting this reaction, inasmuch as it can miss anything, which is technically not at all. And yet. The boy on the roof doesn't even know it's there. He's just sitting on the container, looking up at the sky.

And well should he. Only a nearly microscopic fragment of the probe array is out in the open, and the whole thing's in stealth mode, fully cloaked. It's visible only in ultraviolet, well beyond the range of human eyes to see.

Which does little to explain why the main body of the array has made it maybe two inches out of hiding before the boy on the roof startles up by about one-quarter of a millimeter and then *disappears*.

30.

06 IS DREAMING.

In her dream, she is back at the Comforts of Home Megastore, shouldering up to that clearance rack as if it's insulted her (admittedly, mostly forgotten) parents and then challenged her to single combat to the death. She's loading up her cart like a person who has cash on hand and won't have to triage eleven-twelfths of her food back onto the shelf when she hears a noise, faint but not so faint that 06's company ears can't zero in on it with laser guidance. It's coming from the back of the second shelf up from the floor.

Her dreaming mind says: squirrels. The same ones who looted their food stash last night. They've come here to cut 06's supply off at the source. This leaves her with a quandary. She's still regulating the output of strength from her hands and doesn't want to damage the squirrels in the catching. (In preparation for disaster relief efforts, which score *superlatively* high on marketing models, the Director's been having the operatives practice on white lab rats, picking them up without shattering their bones or splooting their insides out through their mouths. It's a work in progress.)

So, with some trepidation, 06 sinks down on her bootheels, peers in. The good news is: there aren't squirrels back there at all. The bad news is: what is back there is poor, dead 17, by dream-logic in the process of dying all over again. He turns his cheek to the cold metal shelf and regards 06 steadily while blood runs out his eye. The sound she heard was his fingernails scraping at the side of a case of instant ramen she decided against buying yesterday, having no water in which to cook it and no bowl from which to eat.

06's optimistic idiot dream-brain says: *find bandages.* But there aren't any. She pats down her pockets but all she finds is an apparently endless supply of energy bar wrappers, sticky with melty chocolate smears—*All the vitamins and minerals a growing child needs!*

But because she's 06, and 06's chronic inability to be a passive bystander will make Marketing perk up its ears within her first solid month in the field—no easily-classified operative persona needs to be invented for this one, she'll be doing their work for them really—she slaps those wrappers on wherever she sees blood until, an eternity later, 17 is covered in shiny silver and a hundred happy cartoons of his own smiling face.

Once she realizes he's dead, she notices something else. On the side of that case of ramen, 17's scratched out a message in the blood running from the ruptured beds of his nails. It says: *he will be your death.*

06 wakes: gasping, freezing, alone. She can't see

through the corrugated steel of the container roof, but she can see the fading heat signature of 22's presence as the cold saps it away. Later, analyzing the dream, she'll realize the scratching she heard was probably 22 slipping off the roof, dream-time out of sync with real time as per usual. He's been gone seconds at most.

She pushes the container door open and finds 22 along a far wall, near some kind of dead bush, pinching something tiny between one gloved thumb and forefinger with an exactitude of force output calibration that would make the Director proud.

31.

THE PROBE ARRAY resolves at once to update its database: *some children can see in ultraviolet, turns out. And also they can move really,* really *fast.*

32.

IT TAKES 06 AND 22 a few minutes to figure out what to do with the thing. They're both operating under the reasonable and accurate suspicion that this tiny glowing speck, whatever it is, has something to do with the theft of their supplies the night before, which means—however unlikely—it is a tiny glowing speck with the capability of melting a hole in an actual steel wall. That being the case, they can't just leave 22 holding it (as 06 suggests), or trap it in a coffee cup (as 22 would strongly prefer). Eventually they settle on bringing it into the container with them, on the logic that it will (hopefully) take longer to melt through steel (again) than styrofoam, which gives them a window, however small, in which to stop it before it gets away.

"There was more of it," 22 points out. He lifts his chin north-northeast, toward where the late yellow-lit windows of a high-rise still, for all the Director's meddling in their heads, elicit in both children a resilient if vague sense of nostalgia. "It went that way."

Not toward company HQ. Not toward the Director. They don't know what this means but it's interesting.

Who is it reporting to? A bit of surveillance, perhaps, for Greenleaf Industries. Or, maybe worse still, a third-party newsfeed. The size of the thing suggests nanodrone, but those are proprietary Stellaxis IP, much like the two children hustling the violet-blue speck into the illusory safety of the container and shutting the cargo doors securely behind. They'd already know about it. Wouldn't they?

33.

06 PACES in the dark while 22 stares at the speck with folded arms. Out of the light pollution of the city it looks more than ever like a firefly, except smaller, and it's not even trying to take to the air. It's sitting where 22 put it, on the floor of the container, gently pulsing but otherwise inert. The very picture of innocence.

06 furrows her brow. "How much more?" She says this out of nowhere, contextless, but 22 is 22 and 06 is 06 and he knows what she means before she's even finished saying it, maybe before she's finished formulating the thought in her head. That, and there aren't a lot of other super pressing topics of conversation at going on four in the morning when they'd both really rather be asleep.

22 unfolds his arms to gesture, still not taking his eyes off the thing. Trying not to mentally revisit how lucky a person must be, when recklessly grabbing something that can, via methods not readily apparent, *melt steel*, to walk out of that encounter with all his fingers intact.

"And blue like this?"

He nods.

The furrow deepens. "Not exactly inconspicuous."

"Excuse me," says the speck on the floor, causing both children to jump. "Please put that down," it adds, and it's a second before 22 realizes that at some point during this jump he's leapt the whole way to his feet and removed a boot, which he is currently holding aloft in one hand like he's got the mother of all spiders to squash. 06 side-eyes him until he replaces the boot on his foot and sits back down.

"Thank you," says the speck on the floor. "As I was—"

"Hold up," 06 says. "You can *talk*?"

"No," says the speck. It pauses a beat, then adds: "That was sarcasm, which I also cannot do."

22 folds his arms tighter, bodily holding in abeyance the reflex to pick this thing up and maybe pinch a little harder this time. Audibly, ribs creak.

"As I was saying. I'm *supremely* inconspicuous. It's not my fault nobody informed me you can see beyond the baseline human range. Absent that kind of intel, one reasonably tends to assume the—" The glow flickers. "Hang on. I'm curious. How about now?"

The speck shifts out of ultraviolet into something functionally invisible, but its matching of the container's ambient temperature is off by about a twentieth of a degree, which lights it up in infrared, and both children nod.

"Well," it says. "Crap."

06 squints at it. "What *are* you?"

"Doesn't matter what it is," 22 says. "It stole from us." Then, to the speck, with as much misguided imperiousness as a twelve-year-old's outrage and confusion can summon: "The Director sent you, I assume."

"I'm not supposed to say," the speck says. "In fact, I'm not supposed to be interacting with you at all. Statistically, though, ninety-nine-point-six-five-nine percent of me is *not* interacting with you in any way and never has and never plans to, which means that *I*, as a gestalt entity, technically—" It breaks off. "Actually. Speaking of. Can you just, like, look over there for a second?"

"Over where?" 06 asks, at the same time 22 says, flatly: "No."

"Oh, come on," the speck says. "It'll be cool. It's a surprise. But if you look at it, then you'd be by definition interacting with the rest of me, which is something I was expressly instructed to avoid, and this is a very useful loophole for me to have discovered, as you'll see for yourselves if you just give me like five seconds of not looking at that door."

06 and 22 exchange a glance. 06, on whose moral compass *I wanted to see what would happen* is one of perhaps three fixed points, turns her head away while keeping her eyes open and the door in her peripheral vision.

22 is a harder sell. "You didn't answer my question."

"You never asked me one," the speck says primly. "You made an assumption at me. It's not the same thing."

"Are. You. Working. For. The. Director."

"No," the speck says. "I'm decommissioned. I only just met—"

"Did she *send you here* to *steal from us.*"

The speck is silent for a second. "You are property of Stellaxis Innovations. What belongs to you belongs to Stellaxis Innovations. As such you cannot be stolen from."

22 looks about ready to take that boot off again, but 06 tags in. "But the company can," she says. "Stellaxis Innovations. Be stolen from."

"Of course," the speck says.

"Then did you steal our food and money from the company?"

"No."

"Because you didn't take it, or because you took it with company permission?"

"Yes."

"*Which one.*"

"Did you," 22 cuts in with exaggerated patience, "come *here*"—stabbing his pointer finger toward the floor—"last night—to remove things—from this place—while we"—outsize back-and-forth gesture to encompass both 06 and himself—"were sleeping."

"Yes," the speck says.

Both children sit up a little straighter.

"Why?" 06 asks.

"Because I was instructed to."

"By the Director," 06 says darkly. At her side, 22 sits crisscross applesauce, gripping his knees, his spine making a perfect ninety-degree angle with the floor, daring the speck with every iota of his person to even *think* about bullshitting its way out of this.

One-tenth of a second elapses, during which the speck reads the room.

"We were not formally introduced," it says, too airily. "In fact, funny story, I'd been—"

"Enough," 22 says. There's a hematoma quietly developing in his right knee, where he's ruptured a blood vessel. He lifts his hands away. "Get out."

"Wait," 06 says. "What if it can help us?"

"Help us," 22 breathes back, exasperated, "do *what*."

"I don't know. I just—" 06 turns her face down to the speck on the floor. "Give us a minute?"

The speck twitches. It might have been a shrug.

06 drags 22 to the back of the container. "It's too useful to let it get away."

22, dubious insofar as regards their ability to *let* a mystery object that can, to repeat, *melt steel*, do or not do anything, raises one eloquent eyebrow, which 06 ignores. "It's a machine, right?" she says. "It works for the Director, but it's a machine. A computer. Maybe it can be . . . reprogrammed?"

"Do you know how to do that?" 22 asks, only half-sarcastic. It's 06. Maybe she does. "I don't."

"No," 06 says. "But it's not a normal computer. Unless . . ." Her face clouds over.

Unless computers have changed a lot since the Director took us. How would we know?

"You want to . . . talk to it."

"Reason with it. Negotiate with it. Convince it to help us and not her. Yes."

"I don't trust it. It's reporting back to the Director *right now*. She's watching us talk about how we're going to sabotage her sabotage. She's drinking coffee with her feet up on her desk. Guaranteed."

06 pulls a face. "Please."

(Meanwhile, three blocks away, the Director blinks,

puts her coffee down, lowers her feet slowly to the floor.)

22 folds his arms. He can't tell 06 about the Director's voice in his head. Can't share with 06 his line of reasoning: if the Director can do this, she can do anything. Nothing exceeds her reach. Nothing escapes her grasp. Even their little adventure here is built upon the historically shaky bedrock of company tolerance. They should have been engaged with by now in an official capacity. Or black-bagged in their sleep by the more compliant of their fellow operatives. Or bombed.

All at once the realization hits 22 like a bucket of ice water to the face: *she's playing chess with us.* 22, who hasn't the faintest inkling how to play chess himself, has seen enough movies that the concept of chess-game-as-metaphor remains indelibly etched on some useless fold of his brain.

The fact that this—not the color of the walls of his room, not his favorite book, not the faces of his family, but this stupid cliché—has been permitted to stake and hold a claim in the wasteland of his memory, infuriates him so sublimely it literally takes his breath away. His field of vision slews and darkens. Then 06 is shaking him by one shoulder, hard enough to rattle his molars.

He struggles to blink her into focus, but she's blurry, her edges indistinct, backlit somehow. His implant's got some kind of glitch? But he took his lenses out . . .

He feels weird. Unsettled. Feverish, almost. Like he's barely attached to himself anymore, and one wrong move would slough him loose, shake whatever's left of him away.

"Hey," 06 is saying from some vast distance, voice sharpened with concern. "Hey."

By sheer force of will, he dials her in. But her form won't hold. 06 shimmers ominously around the edges, like she's going to burst into fractals, the way a tree or river or artery will branch, and then its branches branch, and then those branches' branches branch again . . .

"I want it gone," he pronounces, slushily. "I do not want it here."

06 narrows her eyes at this. Melodrama is not really 22's style, but the timing of this—what looks to be some kind of imminent fainting spell—is highly suspect. She angles her head at him like a hawk's. "We'll flip for it," she says, watching him carefully as she produces a coin from what is probably a pocket but to 22's compromised higher functions may as well have been the air. Then, magnanimously: "Call it."

"I don't care," 22 says. "This is stupid. That thing is going to destroy us."

"Tails, then," 06 replies. She flips. Both children watch the quarter's upward trajectory. It doesn't embed itself in the container ceiling—she's been practicing—it doesn't so much as brush the flaking rust. It drops through the dark and lands neatly on the back of 06's left glove.

Tails.

"Out," 22 says. His teeth are chattering. It's the Director doing this. The Director's voice in his head. His body is rejecting her intrusion like an organ transplant. The way poor dead 17's body rejected four consecutive livers inside three weeks before the end.

For a moment it seems obvious that the speck will ignore them. They didn't program it to come here. They have no authority to bypass its directive.

But the speck on the floor maybe-shrugs again. "Fair," it says, and without another word floats up and out through an unseen gap between the doors.

Immediately after it vanishes, it pokes the pale blue light of itself back in. "You might want to check outside."

Just past the door something thumps to the ground, and then silence. A moment passes. The speck does not reappear.

06 and 22 exchange a glance. Then, on hands and knees, in total silence, 06 creeps toward the door. Casts one last look over her shoulder at 22, who really doesn't look all that hot right now to be honest. He doesn't warn her against whatever's out there, or tell her to be careful, or anything. He just gazes back at her glassily, like he's been shaken awake from a dream.

06 slides her boots under her, crouched to spring. 22's out of commission, which spins 06's alert readiness up high enough to snap the dial clean off. If they come for her, she'll fight them, sure, but if they come for him, she'll tear a hole in the world with her fucking teeth.

She takes a breath and holds it. Pulls open the door.

On the grass outside is a pizza box, gently steaming in the night air. How it got there is anyone's guess. 06 pans the lot with every trick her considerable visual arsenal possesses. There's nobody around.

34.

THE DIRECTOR doesn't notice the way 06's pulse spikes, then settles, as 06 opens that door braced for violence and finds none. She's preoccupied with 22's vitals. Through the probe array she has eyes on him at this point, and yeah, he doesn't look so great, but he's also been eating out of the trash for two days, it'd be like trying to run a supercar on chocolate syrup and spray cheese. But she knows better.

She stares at the display wide-eyed, frantically gesturing in midair, swiping through readout after readout until she finds one that reassures her.

It never comes.

Fresh in her mind, three years ago like yesterday: 17. Fresher still: 38. She knows exactly what she's looking at. That's what scares her.

35.

MEANWHILE, 06 does what she was created to do. She readies herself for war.

She has no weapons except herself. No plan beyond: hold these doors against whatever comes to breach them. Let none get past her in one piece.

She'd spent a moment debating: open doors or closed? Closed suggests: security, secrecy. But secrecy is a ship that's sailed, and the security is herself. Open gives her a commanding view of about 20 percent of the gate to the lot, upward of 40 percent of the lot itself, as long as she angles her head just right. Anything that breaches that gate, anything that descends from the sky, anything that erupts from the dirt, will have to go through her.

At her back, buried under a hill of coats and scarves, only his face protruding, 22 half sleeps, his mind skipping across the surface of its fever dreams like a stone. Periodically the stone sinks, his breathing deepens, becomes more erratic, bringing 06 up on higher alert, inasmuch as this is possible. Also alarming: he hasn't touched his half of the mystery pizza. 06, stomach grumbling, deliberately does not look at it. He'll be fine after a nap and can eat it then. There is no alternative she cares to entertain. Meantime, its presence—the presence of those calories, the fact of them in her mind—extends her siege. She can't leave for another grocery run, not that she has anything like enough money to bankroll one. She considers trying to summon the weird talking speck back to her—if it brought her food once, maybe it could be talked into doing so again—but tables the idea for now. If 22 was right about it, if the Director sent it, it can't be trusted. Even the pizza had given her pause, though if she's honest, not that great of one. And in the end it hadn't proven, as she'd initially suspected, to be a vehicle for some kind of sleeping drug, administered by the Director to knock her out for easy capture.

On the other hand, she doesn't know what's wrong with 22. Maybe the speck injected him with something, or deployed some type of bioweapon into his airways, and the pizza is there to deflect 06's suspicions. But then why didn't it target her too? It makes no sense.

Something's going to happen. Something's bound to. She just doesn't know yet what. So she kneels before the doors, in total spring-loaded stillness, awaiting trouble, as at her back 22 thrashes and mumbles his way through some unknowable dreamscape.

Any minute now, he'll wake and tell her where he's been. That's the way it's always gone between them: if there is an unseen tether connecting them, in dreams is where it's longest stretched. They talk about them over breakfast, usually, or in their ten daily minutes of unscheduled free time, and in so doing each is in each other's dreams included. To wake and loop 06 in on his solo journeying would be to expand that journey's narrative to contain her.

But he doesn't, leaving 06 feeling like she is peering at the shuttered windows of a house that should have opened to her presence on the doorstep but has not. Instead he burns and twitches, fever pouring from his skin, as he walks some road she can't begin to follow, toward some end beyond the scope of her protection.

06 deeply wants to wake him, just to see if he's okay. But she doesn't. Instead she stares down the doors. Beyond them: faint nighttime city sounds. A drone sighs past en route to somewhere. A block away, three adults argue. Muted 4 a.m. traffic slips by their lot, oblivious. The first sleet patters down. The lack of company goons remains too obvious: what are they waiting for?

For the first time since this all began, she regrets not bringing her sword.

36.

THE DIRECTOR'S sleep deprivation has ranged by now well beyond the uncomfortable, through the false second-wind stage of wakefulness, and on into a kind of stupor, in which she feels dazed and buzzed simultaneously, with an ominous feeling like her eyeballs are gently vibrating, which strikes her as a precursor to nothing good.

She has to sleep. Has to. Can't. It's worse now than before. The removal and destruction of the children's lenses—and the fact that the probe array has for some incomprehensible goddamn reason *left the container*—does nothing to prevent the Director from seeing clearly, in her mind's eye, 06 standing guard over sickly 22. Pacing the container like a caged tiger, perhaps, or crouched on the roof like some annihilating angel. The details are immaterial, a distraction from the crux of the imminent catastrophe. 06 is on the premises, somewhere, lying in wait in the dark, distressingly calm, her pulse and breathing flattened to near nil, readying the machine of herself for the ambush. If she was dangerous on the run, she's infinitely more so backed into a corner, knowing full well she is the only thing that stands between the company and a suddenly defenseless 22. A 22 whose system is on the brink of total collapse, à la 17, à la 38. Once is a tragedy. Twice has the plausible deniability of coincidence. Three times is, as far as the Director's future is concerned, apocalyptic.

She has to retrieve him. Get him into Medical. See if a total blood transfusion and a couple organ transplants will meet with more than the partial success they've been finding in 38 these past few months.

But first 06 must be dealt with. Somehow neutralized or else lured out into the open so that 22 might be nabbed behind her back. While the Director isn't sure which of these options seems least likely, one thing is abundantly clear to her. Whoever she sends into that vacant lot at this point, she's sending in to die.

She's already considered and discarded the idea of reaching out to 06 directly via her implant, the way she failed to do earlier with 22. That's not a bridge she's ready to burn yet, not where 06 is concerned. Mentally the Director pockets this idea: a last resort.

But if there are better options, options that don't end in a bloodbath and seventy-two solid hours of news coverage and the Director packing up her desk into a single cardboard box, they're not apparent. She pictures walking the few blocks to the vacant lot, waving a white lab coat on a stick as a flag of surrender. A lab coat she'd have to borrow, of course, because 06 stole hers. And borrowing means lying, and indebtedness, and suspicions. The Director sighs, drops her head into her hands, does not raise it until she hears the tapping at her window.

The probe array. It's returned.

The Director cracks the window, watches the probe array swirl in and settle on its charging surface in a weirdly pointed-feeling silence. It's vaguely bird-shaped now, vaguely dinosaur-shaped, fluffing its pseudofeathers as it uptakes power from the tray. The Director reminds herself that this thing is an artifact of a program that had its funding cut ages ago, has lived in a box on a shelf in storage for years, and nobody would miss it if it didn't turn up there tomorrow. And it already knows the lay of the land, has already made—and survived—contact with the operatives, and, most importantly, should it stumble into misadventure courtesy of an enraged 06, there would be no blood on the Director's hands. The shelved probe array is expendable, first; second, its existence is not widely known. Their whole alliance is untraceable.

Even with all its nanoparticles combined, the probe array can't bodily remove 06 from the container, the Director knows. She's already made the calculations and discarded them. 06 is too heavy, too uncooperative, too *conspicuous.* An operative being borne away against her will across the night by a boxful of classified experimental space tech is not the level of subtlety the Director hopes to achieve.

However. It was designed to be resourceful, and it has already proven itself to be tricky. As resourceful as 06, who once spent a solid week going back and forth between the operatives, the guards, the techs, the Director's personal staff, etc., in order to barter her way up from a pocketful of hoarded cookies to (god knows how because the Director to this day does not) a secondhand hover-bike that would have almost definitely gotten her and/or 22 killed if the Director hadn't managed to swoop in at the last minute and confiscate it? Or as tricky as 06, who somehow did all this completely under the Director's nose, and probably would have gotten away with her joyride entirely if 28 hadn't narced on her? The Director wouldn't take those odds. But with 22 laid low, 06 will be desperate, clumsy, off her game. Maybe—the Director just about dares hope—susceptible.

It's the best—and, if she's honest, only—play she's got.

37.

IN HIS NEST, 22 sleeps. Wakes. Drifts a little, in between, before sinking again. Everything hurts. Pain drills down into him, dredging up forgotten, half-formed things. If his memory is flotsam, the fever is a hand that rearranges its wreckage into a shoal of trash that holds his weight. Mentally he steps across, gingerly. A couch. Soup. Cartoons. The same sensations he feels now: simultaneously freezing and sweating, weightless and leaden, nauseous and faint with hunger. A shadow is cast over him, someone is crossing his field of vision, someone is switching off the cartoon on the smartwall and telling him to sleep. A parent? A sibling? It's a body made of shadow, its face just north of the top edge of his visual field. He tries to shift his head but it's so heavy. And then the person walks away.

22 opens his eyes, half expects to remain on the far side of that memory. He's on the couch, soup cooling on a nearby table, and all he has to do is open his mouth and call the person back into the room, to sit beside him and let him look upon their face.

Maybe he finds the words, maybe the fever snatches

them away. Whatever noise comes out of him, across the room the person turns to shoot him a look of raw concern over one shoulder.

It's 06, he's back in the container, and the only thought that reaches him with anything like clarity is this: whatever the company sends against them—soldiers, drones, gas, mechs, their fellow operatives, tactical nukes, etc.— 06 has drawn a line in the sand and she's not going to shift an inch.

The only reason his brain can pull this thought up along the frayed rope of itself is: if it were 06 sick in a nest of coats and 22 at the door, he wouldn't do a damn thing different.

Which is why he has to stop her.

If he could just get up and go over there. If he could just talk her out of it. If he could just tell her: *I'm a lost cause. Leave me here and run.*

If he could just keep his eyes open.

He dreams that same dream on loop. *She's the blade that holds the blood in.* Every time he pulls it free of his flesh, it disintegrates into nothing at the precise rate it takes him to bleed out.

38.

A BATTLE—now that's something 06 can handle. It'll be familiar. Refreshing, almost. The closure of it. Just having something *happen*. The calm is suspicious. The waiting sucks. And 22 is scaring the shit out of her.

Clear in her mind, all too clear even three years later, is the last time she saw 17 alive. Crying himself to sleep, pillowcase red and sodden with his tears. 06 had started screaming for a tech to come in and help him, had been brushed off with some story about allergies. They were looking into it. He'd be better in the morning.

But in the morning they'd already taken him away, soggy pillowcase, bed, IV drip, and all, and none of this had at any point reappeared.

Reading her thoughts, perhaps, 22 chooses this moment to swim up to wakefulness. There he treads water for a moment before being sucked back down into the fever dark. "I think I'm dying," he says. "Like 17. You have to get out of here before you catch it."

Like 17, 06 knows, is shorthand for *17 and the three dozen others before him who didn't make it through the first year of treatment.* Still, she takes his point. And ignores it.

"It's just the flu," she says. "There were germs on the garbage. And then you sat outside all night in the cold . . ."

06 trails off, ashamed, having caught a good whiff of her own bullshit. The worst part is she knows 22 knows she's lying, is just too weak to argue. That, more than anything, threatens to send her into spiraling panic.

He needs meds. She knows that much. Not that meds did much to save 17 or the others before him, and she's skeptical that whatever they had 17 on for that last week while he was wired up to all those tubes will be anything she can buy for sidewalk change at the Comforts of Home Megastore. Or steal there, for that matter, so there goes her next idea. She already knows that 38 received whole new organs down at Medical, because 38 likes to show off the scars. And 06 is pretty sure they don't sell human livers on ice at Comforts of Home, and if they did, she sure as hell doesn't know how to transplant one into 22. It's beyond infuriating. No matter how far they run, how long they last, how much they thrive beyond the boundary of company HQ, they carry the company with them, and it will always, always win.

She's going to feel pretty stupid if this turns out to just be a cold.

In the meantime, though, if she's right, and whatever mystery company sickness that got 17 and those before him has burrowed into 22, then sitting and waiting is an almost guaranteed death sentence. Besides, it's just about the furthest possible thing from her style. The absence of a solid plan of action feels like fingernails scrabbling at the inside of her skull. She wants to scream frustration out into the night, go out there and punch holes in the side of a building, twist a car in half and pitch it over- hand above the skyline toward company HQ—but can't allow herself to break down in front of 22. Whether he's lucid enough to register it or not. Which seems increas- ingly unlikely.

She doesn't realize she's holding the edge of the con- tainer until she feels the metal buckling in her hands. She lets go, blinking hard.

And remembers the speck. They'd kicked it out, but to be fair they hadn't invited it in the first place. Maybe it hasn't gone far.

"Hey," she whispers as softly as she can, knowing full well that if 22 is so much as half-awake he'll assume, ra- tionally, that she's talking to him. But he sleeps on, a coat sleeve thrown over half his face, the exposed skin waxy and lucent with fever, brow creased as he navigates some maze of a dream.

"I'm not sure," he mumbles, not to her, and flings his left arm out, totally insensate. It's stopped by the wall, leaving a divot the size of a plate. Distressingly, he does not wake.

06 leans a little farther out into the night and tries again. "Psst. Hey."

"I heard you the first time," says a voice from what feels like *inside her ear*, and 06 suppresses the urge to stick her finger in there and scratch. "Are you going to kick me out again?"

Unsaid here, 06 knows, is: *and how well did that work out for you last time?*

"He's sick," 06 says. "I don't know what's wrong," she tries to add, but her voice catches on *wrong*. She knows. At least, she knows enough.

"Hmm," says the voice.

Millions of dollars have been spent on the rewiring of the operatives' senses until they are virtually indistinguishable from magic. Still, 06 registers not so much as a tickle as the speck removes itself from her ear and glides down to situate itself on her knee. More specks swirl in from outside and they gather in a mass that forms, nearly instantaneously, into a tiny octopus. It lifts one arm at her in greeting. "This okay?"

"It's fine," 06 says, because what else can she say? She has no idea what this thing is, where it came from, if it can hurt them, if she could hurt it if she had to, if it can be trusted. The thought that more specks could be swimming around in her bloodstream, or 22's—that it could be what *made him sick*—while disconcerting, is swiftly discarded. Had it not been for 17's decline, a spectacle that the remaining eleven children all personally witnessed, the idea would have far more sticking power. As it is, whatever this thing is, it brought them pizza, did not try to gas them, seems friendly enough, and the pizza didn't seem to be laced with any toxins beyond the usual freight of growth hormones and microplastics, etc.

Right now it's the closest thing to an ally she has.

"Do you have diagnostic capabilities? Medically, I mean?"

The octopus sniffs. "Not to brag, but diagnostic capabilities are kind of my whole—"

"I need to know what kind of medicine to get him."

It *hmm*s a little. Then it levitates off 06's knee, turns sideways in midair, all eight arms radially extended, and cartwheels its way over to where 22 has now interred himself entirely in his coat nest. There it lowers down to, but does not land on, the one square centimeter of skin that remains exposed. It hovers for a moment, humming to itself as it tastes the air. 06 looms behind it, daring it with her eyes. But it doesn't try anything funny. At least not that she could prove.

The whole process lasts maybe five seconds. Then it climbs the air until it's at eye level with 06. "May I?" it says, extending an arm toward her shoulder. It takes a seat on her responding shrug.

"So what's wrong with him?" 06 asks it.

"Well," the octopus says. "First thing you need to know about me is I've been in storage for longer than you've probably been alive, and it looks like there's a lot of interesting stuff I missed out on. I barely know what *he* is, let alone which of my readings differ from whatever his baseline is, and how. His data's abnormal. *He's* abnormal. Maybe if someone had thought to take me out of storage at some point over the past decade, I might have—"

In a flash of inspiration, 06 blurts: "Compare him to me."

"What?"

If 06 didn't know better, she'd think this *what* sounded less like *I didn't quite catch that* and more like *I'm taken aback that this conclusion reached you before me.*

"The readings. The data. Do whatever you did to him, to me, and see what's different."

The octopus stretches waaaay up on the tips of its arms in order to regard 06 levelly. "You feel healthy?"

"Hundred percent," 06 declares, suppressing the urge to flex a little in illustration. She's running at more like eighty, ninety max, but that's mostly to do with how her whole metabolic system is a high-performance balancing act with no net and it's not designed to function on trash-can donuts and congealed pizza and no sleep. "Read me."

"All right." The octopus tiptoes over to an exposed stretch of neck and hangs out there for a second, doing absolutely nothing 06 can discern. She's not really sure what she expected. Beeping, maybe. Sniffing. Something. But the next thing she knows there's a series of readouts being projected holographically in midair before her. Two series of readouts, side by side. They are not remotely identical.

"I won't bore you with the details," the octopus says, "but yeah, no, you're right, he's seriously jacked up. He needs medical attention."

06 runs her hands back through her hair in frustration. "I can get to the store in a few minutes if I go over the roofs," she mutters to herself. "I'll probably have to steal the meds."

"Crime?" the octopus squawks. "On my watch? What kind of a chaperone would I be if—"

"Look who's talking! *You* took our money. The other night. Don't bother denying it, I know it was you."

"Who said anything about denying it?" the octopus

replies. "In fact, look up if you want to see something cool."

06, chronically deprived these past few years of sights she would describe as *cool*, looks up and out through the open doors. From a nearby rooftop, coins drift down to her on some unseen conveyance. She opens her hand and holds it out, and $8.91 stacks itself neatly on her palm.

It's more than the thing stole from them to begin with. Still, with sinking heart, 06 knows it's not enough. Not near. But it's a start.

"Thank you," she says, and means it.

"Oh, that?" the octopus says airily. "That was the distraction."

"What?"

"Check your pocket."

06 sets her handful of change on the container floor, then shoves both hands into the pockets of her lost-and-found coat. Nothing.

"No, your other pocket."

She lifts her butt to check her pants pockets. Nothing.

"No, your *other* other pocket."

"I don't have a—" 06 begins, then realizes. She unzips the lost-and-found coat to get at the pockets of the stolen lab coat beneath. There, impossibly, in the chest pocket, is a wad of bills. She pulls it out and stares. She's never held so much money before in her life.

"Cool trick, huh?" the octopus says, in a tone that strongly suggests it does not need something so immaterial as 06's opinion to validate it. "Well? What are you waiting for?"

Because 06 has jumped to her feet, shut the doors at her back, taken three bounding steps out of the container—and, upon realizing the octopus has resumed its position on her shoulder, stopped like someone's hit pause on her. Wordlessly she half turns, looks back at the silent shape of the container, chewing her lower lip. "Could you just," she asks, her tone very different from any the probe array—whether speck or octopus or flying carpet or anything—has heard from her yet, "just stay here and keep an eye on him for me? Until I get back?"

It's been a long time since a child has trusted the probe array, and forever since *anyone* has trusted it with a task of such obvious import to the asker. If it were susceptible to anything as messy as human emotion, this is the part where it might tear up a little.

As it is, it is mercifully immune. At least mostly. So instead it reaches out one tiny arm, curls the endmost quarter of it into something like a fist, and boops 06 on the cheek. "Biped," it tells her, "I'm way ahead of you."

06 peeks over a shoulder and sees an identical octopus, a little smaller than hers, perched on 22's forehead. It lifts an arm and gives her a miniature salute.

"See?" says 06's octopus. "All good."

But 06 does not see, not really, and is suddenly second-guessing her request. Whatever this thing is, it's connected to Stellaxis. Has to be. Or else to Greenleaf. It's here to gather intel on them. Maybe. Which might not be as bad. In her current state of mind, which is frantically spinning desperation into optimism, it even feels more likely. If it were Stellaxis, something would have happened by now.

She'd be ripping into a whole battalion barehanded, or dueling 28 or 33 to the death in this shitty trash-strewn lot. (The lot's trash-strewn again, she realizes. Has 22 been out that long? Or has it just been super windy? Her sense of time, of proportion, of everything, is shot.)

That turns out to be what decides for her. This weird whatever-it-is tech might be a spy, but it doesn't seem to be an enemy. After all, it gave her money. It's helping her help 22. The Director wouldn't tell it to do those things, nobody at Stellaxis would, but someone at Greenleaf might, if they were trying to lure two enemy operatives into turning. A healed 22's going to be worth more to them than a dead one. And then he and 06 can fight their way out of whatever next mess they land themselves in together.

06 nods to herself, once, and squares herself against the night. "Let's go."

39.

IN THE DIRECTOR'S OFFICE, one segment of the probe array has stayed behind, humming two-decades-out-of-date commercial jingles to itself on its charger as the Director paces laps around her desk. Now, an interminable time later, it finally shuts up. The sudden silence is enough to turn the Director on her heel so fast she rolls her ankle, but just a little. She can still walk. She can still run. She couldn't outrun the operatives if it came to that, of course, but in the best shape of her life she couldn't either. If death comes for her tonight, she takes comfort in the fact that it'll be swifter than she'll see arriving.

Waiting for intel, she's got her winter coat on, a floofy scarf, and a nice, anonymizing ball cap. That's insufficient too, she knows. There aren't enough coats and hats and cozy accessories in the world to hide her from the sublime apparatus that is 06. No, they will meet in single combat, as if foretold in some old prophecy, and one of them will fall.

Which is to say: she's going to ambush 06 out of the Comforts of Home with a tranquilizer ampoule, rare and precious, tailored to 06's metabolic profile. In the

Director's pocket: 22's. They are experimental, one of a kind, not yet fully tested, utterly bespoke. She has no idea what will happen, had been really hoping it wouldn't come to this. And yet it has. The costume is there to buy her the split second she needs to fire one into 06's center of mass before 06 feeds the Director her own spine. Best-case scenario.

"Now?" she asks, a little breathless. Anticipation or fear? She can't tell.

And the probe array lifts in response a tiny, perfectly formed, all the more horrifying for its blitheness, jauntily neon-blue thumbs-up.

40.

She's the blade that holds the blood in.
    She's the blade that holds the blood in.
    She's the blade that holds the blood in.

22 has lost count of the number of times he's pulled that knife out and exsanguinated himself on the Director's shiny shoes. Each time, the next try will wake him up. Has to. Refuses to. Stupid to think he could break free of it, the cling and sough and undertow of it. That he could outsmart it. Outsmart himself. When what he is is gone.

She's the blade that holds—

He pauses, hand wrapped around the hilt of the broken sword.

And lets go.

The Director smiles at him and begins to burn. Around the edges, like an eclipse. Then the flame eats inward. *You can never truly know a person*, the Director whispers, steam coming out of her mouth, and smiles at him, mockingly, as the gobs of fire that are herself drop away.

It will be years before he realizes who she means. And by then it will be too late.

For now, he walks out of that unfamiliar room, and

he closes the door behind him, and the shadow he casts as he walks down the hall is rough-edged, the shape of a thing crudely broken, and his footsteps are fire, but the blade holds his blood in as promised, not forever, but at least for as long as it takes for him to walk down that hall and into an elevator and for the doors to whish shut behind him and this time, a hundred thousand million iterations in—he wakes.

He wakes, and the fever hasn't broken, but he's pushed it back a little, like he's swum up from deep water to find a tiny pocket of air. He's covered in cold sweat. His mouth tastes like neat death. And there's a little blob sitting on his chest.

It doesn't look like anything in particular, but he knows immediately what it is. Something about the sentry position it's assumed there keeps him from sitting up, from saying anything. He feigns sleep through slitted eyelids, scoping out the lay of the land.

It's dark. The doors are cracked an inch for air circulation. There's half a cold pizza on the floor. Of 06, or of any clue to her whereabouts, there is no sign.

"Morning, sunshine," says the thing on his chest. "Nice attempt, but I'm kind of sitting directly on top of your heartbeat, so."

22 sits up, dislodging it. It floats beside him. "Where is she?" he asks it.

"Running errands," it tells him. "She told me to make sure you got your beauty rest."

This strikes 22 as insultingly un-06-like. He shivers, not from fever. "She said that?"

In response the thing plays 06's voice at him, saying, yes, exactly that. Word for word, in fact. "See?" it adds in its own bee-swarm voice, smirkly.

It's 06's voice, all right. But it's not 06. Despite that he's never heard 06 utter the phrase "beauty rest" in his life, something about the intonation's off. He can't quite place it. It sounds like someone's stuck their hand up 06's back, wearing her like a puppet. It hits like someone's dumped a bucket of spiders down the back of his shirt.

It's not her.

He swats the thing out of the air. It hits the far wall, stunned, and begins to slide down. 22 gets there first. He grabs it in one fist and squeezes.

"Oh, come on," the thing says, muffled by fingers. "I thought that was pretty solid."

"*Where is she.*"

The thing oozes out of 22's grasp, reforms on the back of his hand. Now it looks like a miniature 06. "I told you," the thing says in her voice. "I'm out running errands. Go back to sleep."

"She wouldn't leave me," he says, sounding out the concept like feeling his way into a dark room. "She wouldn't have just *left*."

"Would and did," says the tiny 06. "You're sick. You need meds. Go back to sleep."

Is it his imagination or does the false 06 voice sound a little different now? A little more insistent?

Something's wrong. He feels it. It tingles in his palms. He just doesn't know what it is.

"I'm not tired," he tells it. "Tell me where she went. Tell me how to get there."

"It doesn't matter," it says. "You're supposed to be sleeping. Go back to sleep."

And there, on the third *go back to sleep*, he hears it. The thing's desperation doesn't code as human, because it isn't. But he reads it loud and clear. 06's inflection has peeled away from it like old paint from a house. What's beneath is a directive, which it is failing to attain. It is the closest possible thing to alarm it is capable of expressing, and it is blaring it from all channels right now.

"Why," he asks very slowly, "do you want me to go back to sleep?"

A second passes.

"Beauty rest?" the thing says, and that's all 22 needs to hear. 06 has been compromised. This thing has compromised her. His illness has compromised her, and maybe that's the worst of it. Betrayal he expected, but his own uselessness *grates*. The fact that he could not help her, in the end. That he was deadweight when she needed him. That whatever trouble she's in now, she's facing alone.

22 still feels like reheated shit. What's got ahold of him hasn't let go yet. His pocket of air is dwindling. He can feel the fever encroaching, a huge hand pressing him down.

He digs deep, finds his strength, his speed. What's left of them.

He grabs the thing again.

"Listen to me now," he says. "I know you can shape-change. I don't care. Stab me, burn me, do whatever to me you did to that door, I don't care. Try to escape and I will catch you. Try to stop me and I will break you. I'm going to find her, and you can come with me or stay. But what you're not going to do"—his other hand darts toward it, comes back with a few grams of its nanomaterial pinched between his thumb and forefinger, and he shows it to the thing, makes sure it sees, before he crushes it to dead dust and lets it fall—"is get in my way."

41.

TRYING TO FIND the right meds is worse than trying to buy groceries. 06 has less than no idea what she's doing, and the octopus or speck or whatever it is (it's hiding under her hat, she can't see it) is no help at all. It gives her no decisive intel. She's holding up one brightly colored package after another and pretending to study it long enough for the thing to poke from the open knit of the hat what 06 envisions as an eyestalk but probably is not and then whisper in her ear a yes or no. Which seemed to 06 to be the least efficient possible method for getting this done, but the thing has so far been weirdly averse to doing it any different way.

Wordlessly 06 holds up a blister pack of pills, giving it a little shake for emphasis. She gave up asking questions like "This one?" or "How about this?" approximately seven billion items ago. She fakes squinting at the small print, waiting while the thing prevaricates near her ear, trying to drag her mind by main force into a place of calm, wondering if this is what a person feels like before they spontaneously combust.

"Flip it over," the voice says. "Let me read the back."

Obediently, 06 flips it over. More time passes.

"How's he doing?" she asks. It's either that or chew a hole in her cheek. Or pick up the whole fucking shelf of meds and pitch it through the glass frontage of the store. Or explode.

"You have asked that nine times now."

"Because this is taking forever."

"Do you know you're not the first child who expected me to be a medbot for some reason? I'm doing the best I can. Let me see that one over there."

With difficulty, 06 tries to follow where it's pointing, but she still can't see a finger or eyestalk or tentacle or anything. "What one over where?"

"Take a few steps to your right."

06 complies.

"Your other right."

"You mean my left?"

"Isn't that what I said?"

06 tears off her hat and glowers down at the thing nestled inside. It's mostway into a flash transformation into what looks like possibly a kitten? Something meant to blink up at her with eyes of liquid innocence. But she's too fast, she's caught it off-guard, and it looks more like a kitten drawn by a toddler who's never seen one. Kind of . . . melty. And it's got one too many ears.

06 has spent the past twenty minutes fighting the suspicion that she's being messed with. That this thing, whatever it is, is only playing at being helpful. That it's still the Director's toy, or the other company's, or who-ever's, and all it's trying to accomplish here is exactly

this: 06 in front of this stupid shelf, rummaging through pill bottles all night like a chump, while 22 is entirely unguarded.

All at once, she can't fight it any longer. She's been too naive. Too trusting. And now she's too late.

The thing is quick. But 06 is quicker. She drops the thing, hat and all, and stomps it hard enough to sink it through the fake-tile flooring and three inches of concrete beneath.

Doesn't stick around to see if she was fast enough to break it, or if it had enough time to transform into something unsquishable. She sweeps an armload of meds into her red shopping basket and is out the door before the antitheft sensors can register her passage.

She's four steps out the door when the Director's trank ampoule buries itself in the side of her neck. It's an outrageously lucky shot—most of 06 is padded under various coats, but around her throat she's just got the one thin scarf.

Immediately she registers the attack. Rips the needle from her neck and whirls to zero in on the figure, half-hidden behind an ornamental sidewalk tree, ducking down into its own coat like it's trying to armor itself down to the navel with the brim of its ball cap. Fumbling with some kind of pistol that appears nowhere in 06's extensive mental database of handheld weaponry.

She's got no time. No way to know what she's been shot up with, or by whom. No way to know if a second dose is on the way. No time to temper her response, to crank back her force output. No weapon but the shopping basket, which on pure reflex she hurls at the figure hard enough to put it on its ass, twenty feet behind where it'd been standing, all its internal organs reduced to slurry.

Or . . . it should have. Something stops it. Something barely visible beyond a shimmering like the heat that radiates up off pavement on a summer afternoon. Something that reaches out of the empty air and *catches* the basket in such a way that it does not shatter and also does not disperse its velocity backward into the person who should by rights be pulverized. In such a way, in short, as shouldn't be possible. Something that sets the basket down with a precise little teacup-into-saucer sound, like it's punctuating a point in an argument that 06 has absolutely, comprehensively, irretrievably lost.

Something that 06, grasping after the crumbling handholds of her consciousness on her collision course with oblivion, still has plenty of time to recognize. Both the thing and the figure behind it, now raising its face into the fluorescent light spilling from the storefront, weirdly tilted in a way that 06 takes a second to realise has less to do with the Director's posture and more to do with the fact that 06 is in the process of crashing in slow motion to the sidewalk.

So slow. Everything's so slow. She's 06 and invincible and has all the time in the world to react. Neutralize the Director. Destroy the thing. Gather her spilled meds and get back to 22 before whatever the Director shot her up with can so much as break her stride.

All the time in the world.

It's there, and then it's dwindling, and then it's gone.

42.

FROM A BLOCK AND A HALF AWAY, 22 watches her fall.

43.

THE DIRECTOR'S got no time to waste. Between the probe array and the strength of her own arms, she's got to get 06 out of here before someone notices. She's got a cloaking device ready to drape over the prone form of 06, so nobody's going to be picking up on her visually without several specific and proprietary implant upgrades. It's not perfect, but it buys her the couple of minutes she needs to call up her car from where it's idling in an alley and get 06 wrestled into the trunk.

That done, she'll go back to that godforsaken shipping container and put a dose in 22 before he surfaces from his fever sleep and stops her. Which is the least of her concerns: she's got a subset of the probe array standing sentry over him; it would tell her if anything changes, anything that would shift up her timetable from *emergency* to *catastrophe*. Anyway, she can pull up 22's vitals anytime she chooses, but the outlook's no less grim. That liver's got to go. The kidneys too, probably. A total blood transfusion. It's working on 38 so far, so she's got reason to believe it—

She's midway through racking 22's dose into the

chamber, multitasking while she calls her car up to the curb, when three things strike her with such sudden, nauseating clarity that her heart record-scratches, agonizingly, then reboots.

1. She never specifically told the probe array to inform her if 22 exits the container. If he stops breathing? Yes. If his blood oxygen levels drop into the danger zone? Absolutely. Anything that would suggest the company has flushed another couple hundred million dollars down the toilet and be on the hunt for someone to blame? Of course. But that he might have somehow, from some unthinkable depth, dredged up the strength to drag his three-quarters-dead carcass out of that container and across whole city blocks on foot? No. Because she remembers 17, and she remembers 38, and she knows it's simply not possible.

2. That if she had that to do it over, she would have made better decisions. Because:

3. When she glances up from the trank pistol, there he is. Maybe forty feet away, unarmed, leaning on a wall, looking less like a bleeding-edge superweapon and more like a corpse reanimated by an amateur, and he'll be within her range positively ages before she's within his, and the Director knows, with perfect, awful lucidity, that none of that is about to matter, because he's there and then he's *not*, and then she's on her back and the fluorescent lights of the Comforts of Home are above her and her head feels funny and the trank gun's gone and she goes to gasp and can't.

44.

"Hey," someone is saying. "Hey, kid. Hey."

Effortfully, 22 dials the world into focus. He's on the sidewalk. His knees are cold. Everything hurts. Swathes of bright and dark swing wide around him, pitching queasily. Something tapping on his shoulder, poky and insistent. He goes to brush it away, realizes his hands are occupied. Looks down.

His knees are cold because he's kneeling on the concrete, which is the approximate temperature of the nighttime air, and he's skinned them both, and he's bleeding. His hands are occupied because they're wrapped around the Director's throat.

Some kind of pistol lies beside her, crumpled like a soda can. Scattered around it, spilled from a red plastic shopping basket, are various boxes and blister packs of meds, all kinds of meds. Stuff for fevers, stuff for colds, stuff for flu. Cough drops and eye drops and dermal patches and things he doesn't recognize, like the Comforts of Home vomited up its medicine aisle onto the front walk.

There's a sound coming out of the Director that

he hasn't heard before. Whoever's talking to him, it's pretty definitively not her. Not 06 either—the first and only thing he clocked upon arrival was that she's out but breathing, steady and slow. Tranquilized. Which they have been assured, repeatedly, is not possible. They can't even be gassed. They're superheroes. They're invincible.

At his nine o'clock, a customer strolls out of Comforts of Home, takes one look at whatever's going down out here, and hurries off at top speed. Another follows, blinking to snap a picture on their lenses as they back away. 22 ignores them.

"Kid. Hey. She needs air. And, I mean, you probably know this, but you're impeding her circulation."

Now he recognizes the voice. Feels the barely perceptible weight of the thing on his shoulder. It accompanied him here, not even bothering to try and stop him—showing him the way, even—knowing what he'd find when he arrived.

"Shut up," he grits at it.

"You're mad at me," it says, floating up in front of him. "Listen, I get it. But I had my orders. You of all people should underst—" He glances at it and it shuts up. "Okay, maybe not. But be that as it may. I was just . . ."

22 tunes it out. He's been played. They've both been played. They were never going to walk free. The Director's influence burrows into them, nosing its roots into every part of them, even now.

He looks at the Director. He looks at 06. He ponders the slow collapse of his system, gaining steam with every second.

All he has to do is squeeze. Not hard either. Nothing simpler. What's more surprising to him is that he hasn't done it already. It comes to him that he's got his grip exactly regulated so that the Director hasn't quite blacked out, hasn't quite stopped breathing, but is in a kind of near-death limbo, where she remains at his discretion.

It doesn't even feel good. The power of it. He doesn't want to be touching her, his lost-and-found mittens against the frantic fluttering of her pulse. He doesn't want to be here. He wants to be literally anywhere except here. He wants 06 to get up and help him. Or stop him. Or leave him here and flee. He doesn't know what to do.

He wants to squeeze, like 06 would absolutely have done by now. Wants it to be over. That's all it would take. Just to close his hands a little tighter. Less force than breaking the gun. Way less. She doesn't seem so tall down here, knocked clean out of her heels. That horrible clicking sound coming out of her throat. Her pulse like something trapped. Fragile. Easily crushed.

It's surprising, all things considered. That he should be given this power over her. That he should hate it as much as he does.

Meanwhile: 06 so inert, so still, so unlike herself. Even in her sleep she shifts and kicks and wriggles. He must be hallucinating. The fever. No way can this 06—can any of this—be real.

But it is, she is, and he hasn't the first fucking clue how to undo what's been done to her. How to bring her back to herself.

He may be running a fever of 108, his organs may be

deliquescing, his body may be shutting off its last lights and closing up shop for real, but he's got enough strength left in his hands to kill the Director right here on this sidewalk. And die free.

He realizes this, as he realized it a minute ago, and watches himself realize it from a hazy remove, like he's floating above himself, and goes to close his hands tighter and then watches himself fail to.

Over the years to come he will spend a good long time replaying in his head what he does instead.

22—loosens his grip. Just a little. His sense of time has become desynced from itself, its anchor raised a bit from the collective reality, and he hasn't quite decided to do it before it's done, and the Director is sucking in air.

The Director's not entirely sure why her windpipe hasn't been forcibly interknit with her spine, is fully aware that the window of opportunity for this to happen stands wide, wide open. 22's stare is a weight she can feel palpably, in the base of her gut and the backs of her hands. Panic. What she is feeling now is panic.

She will only get one chance to speak. If she fucks this up, they'll have to run swabs off the sidewalk to ID her.

"She's all right," the Director says at once. "She's okay. She's just asleep."

The stare does not lessen in intensity, but she's still breathing, and honestly at this point that fact lives somewhere beyond *reasonable expectation* and firmly in the realm of *pleasant surprise*.

"Hey, boss," the probe array says. "You want me to do anything here, or . . . ?"

With difficulty, the Director shakes her head. Keeping her eyes on 22 all the while, like: *see? I'm not your enemy. I never was.* Realizing that what she's really doing is stalling. There's no endgame here that she can win. Maybe there's a brilliant idea buried under the muddle of her thoughts, some scenario that might not end with her being liquefied on a sidewalk, but it isn't springing immediately to mind. Blaring over her actual thoughts is the urge, instinctual and undignified, to stay exceptionally still, exceptionally small, exceptionally unthreatening. Like he'll have forgotten for one nanosecond who she is, and what she stands for, and what she's done.

"Okay," the probe array says. "That's actually great because I'm pretty low on power right now. I'll just be over here. Good luck!" And with that, it floats over to glom onto the side of the COMFORTS OF HOME neon sign by the door. The light flickers a little. The probe array sighs happily.

It comes to the Director that there is no good or plausible reason for her to still be alive, but that in order for her to remain so, she needs to keep talking. Give him reasons not to kill her. How the hell he made it all the way out here on his own power without collapsing in a gutter is frankly beyond her. 17 and 38 and the three dozen before them are a burden of memory she'll never quite put down, carved in high relief on the folds of her brain. She should not have to be pleading for her life with 22. He shouldn't be able to move. He should barely be able to *breathe.*

"Nothing in that basket will help you," she wheezes

at him. "Nothing in a thousand stores like this will help you. But I can. If you come back with me. Right. Now."

For a moment 22 is confused at the Director's abrupt switching of gears. Like his own health is his concern here. He's not sure he entirely believes the Director's claims. 06 is visibly drawing breath, but still. That a person like her could be simultaneously so thoroughly extinguished and *okay* is an insult to his intelligence. 06, despite all her efforts, is back in the Director's clutches. Thus, she is, by definition, the furthest possible thing from *okay*.

And 22, simmering in the toxic soup of full-on systemic autolysis, is at this point assailed by what can only be described as an epiphany. Later he will not be able to trace any kind of logical path of it to himself, and by that time it will have been added to the tiny but growing pile of secrets he has kept from 06, along with *so I heard the Director's voice in my head, trying to turn me against you.*

It's not an intellectual thought, what strikes him now. Not something he has reasoned through, meticulously, rationally. It's a bolt from the blue. When the fever breaks he won't even remember it, but it will stay with him, latched on, assimilated, indivisible.

It is as follows, as best as his current state of five-alarm medical emergency allows the thought to form at all: *you can never truly know a person.*

The words strike his mind like a bell, set it ringing with arcane urgency. He grasps after its meaning, frustrated and unsure where he'd heard those words last. The blade from the dream. The Director, burning. But he's awake now.

Isn't he?

And 22, awash in fever, his everything gone haywire, maybe a little unhinged, realizes he understands. Or thinks he does.

You can never truly know a person.

But you can make a person think they truly know you.

Yes, he could kill the Director. Carry 06 out of here. But then what? Back to the shipping container? If the Director knows they were there, the rest of the company does too. Whatever next thing they'd send after them would be worse. Worse still, 06 is down, and as for 22, he's got a pretty solid sense there's something deeply wrong with him. Dilemma: even if he could undo what's been done to 06, she'd never agree to run without him, and the way he is right now he'll only drag her down. And that's not an option he can live with.

So this run's burnt. But they can use what they learned here to regroup and try again. Go farther next time. Faster. Bolder. Better prepared. Take food with them. Warmer clothes. Their weapons. They stand no chance against, say, 28 or 33 or even 05 without them.

They'll do it again. And next time they'll do it right.

Suddenly he knows, as clearly as he knows anything, that he will survive the Director. He will outlast her. A day will come when he'll annihilate her utterly, and she and all her work will be undone, and he'll walk away with 06 at his side and never once look back. Perhaps not today, perhaps not tomorrow, and perhaps not even within his lifetime. But he'll win.

And he'll do it by playing her game.

He's the obedient one? Fine. He can be that.

For a while.

"It's what happened to 17, isn't it," 22 says. Playacting is not his strong suit—yet—but a panicked note is not hard to convey. Even if the Director misunderstands the cause. "What's happening to me."

"Yes," the Director says, naked relief in her voice. It's almost laughable. How obvious her motives. "That's why you need to come with me. So I can get you the help you need."

It's easy. It's too easy. And it will only get easier in time.

He looks down at the Director, her upturned face, her eyes full of light, and almost—almost—smiles.

The Director clears her throat. "You have to know," she ventures after a moment, "all I want is what's best for you b—"

And all at once 22's on his feet, looking down at her, and she's staring up at him, very, very still, because to flinch would be to show weakness, to flag herself as his enemy, and there's no coming back from that.

But he's holding out one randomly mittened hand (where have his gloves gone? she wonders distantly) and she's hesitating only a little before taking it, and they're both steeling their faces, but against the betrayal of very different emotions as, force output calibrated precisely, he pulls her to her feet.

45.

THE DIRECTOR'S feeling pretty pleased with herself, really. She lost them, yes, but she brought them back herself. On her own time. Of their own free will. Well, of 22's free will anyway, but 06 was always going to be a hard sell verging on impossibility. The fact that he came home readily, without fuss, without draing attention, without even a little bit of a massacre, without any of the things the Director had (reasonably) feared? It's a victory beyond her wildest hopes.

The fact that he refused to get into the Director's car, refused to put 06 in it either, refused to so much as touch it for that matter, and insisted on *carrying* 06 all fourteen blocks back to the company lawns and through the black glass doors of HQ himself—less ideal. But she got him to put on the cloaking device first, at least, so they weren't spotted, and by the time they got back it was some ungodly hour of the morning, just AI at the front desk, and neither the Director nor the operatives, being regular occupants of the building, aroused its suspicions. And now they're both snug in Medical. 06's bespoke tranquilizer doesn't seem to have done her any lasting harm, and 22's numbers will hopefully start to look marginally less alarming once he has ten units of someone else's blood in him. She's already woken up the med team and they're en route to get those organs suctioned out and redone.

Even better, it looks like her hypothesis was correct. 06 as flight risk, but 22 as anchor. She hadn't exactly expected a person whose whole biological architecture was snowballing into runaway detonation to be able to do . . . well, if she's honest, any of the things she witnessed. Terrifying in retrospect, considering what he could have done *to her*, but also in retrospect enormously reassuring. Validating, even. Of course the illness helped to sway him, the promise of comfort beneath the company wing, but there is zero doubt in the Director's mind that if 06 had confronted her on that sidewalk and not 22, the Director would be in a hospital right now. If not a morgue. 06 would have let her organs dissolve and run out her pores before giving herself up to the company.

Could 22 have brought 06 in a little sooner? Saved the Director a whole pile of trouble? Not taken quite so many years off her life? Sure. But she's spent full days now at the mercy of her brain regaling her in cinematic detail with all the horrifying ways in which this could all have ended so *incredibly* much worse. Besides, it makes sense he'd want to save face in front of his partnered operative. Pretended to be on her side. Played along with the little adventure. When it came down to it, he showed where his loyalty lies. He could have expunged the Director from the face of the earth. He could have fed her her own car. He could have atomized her utterly and run, and not a force on earth could catch him.

Instead he'd failed to meet the Director's eye and said: *don't tell her.* Meaning 06. Meaning *that I betrayed her.* And then he'd paused. Gathered himself invisibly. Said: *please.*

Of course, the Director had told him. Struggling to hide quite how badly that *please* had startled her. Smiling down, beatific, just stopping herself forcibly from tousling his hair with one trembling hand. *My lips are sealed.* And now she's got all eleven operatives back safe and sound(ish), and all is right with her world.

Best of all, 22 did the right thing in the end. As she'd always known he would.

Tomorrow she'll have them take a look at his implant. Figure out why she couldn't get through to him when she tried. Maybe even do a bit of conferring as to preventative measures. Some kind of implant upgrade that alerts her when her operatives are plotting something nefarious. Or even better: one that punishes them for doing so. A little mental shock collar for rebellious thinking. That ought to do the trick.

But all that is a problem for future-her. As is getting a story in order for when she has to face the other operatives. As is figuring out where exactly the probe array has gone off to. As is getting her adrenaline back down low enough that she can *sleep.*

For now? She's going to take the win.

46.

22 PROBABLY SHOULDN'T BE AWAKE—he's more heading into the woods of his illness than out of them, and anything that could tip the odds in his immune system's favor might make the difference between him walking out of Medical eventually or being carried out in a body bag—but he can't sleep. The fever squats over him, staring eyeless into his face, lowering its weight onto his chest. Every time he thinks it can't get worse, it ratchets down, crushing him to the cot so that he struggles for breath. Whatever's in his IV drip isn't doing anything noticeably helpful at all. Unless it is, and that's the really scary thing, the thought he's staring at the ceiling trying frantically not to have. That without the drip he'd be dead already.

If he's honest, it's not the only thought he's hiding from. Another is: 06. When she wakes up. When she asks him how the Director nabbed him. Because that's the only version of reality that will make sense to her. That he was jumped in his sleep in the container, shot up with the same tranquilizer that dropped 06. A reality where 22 took the Director's side, or seemed to, is incompatible with any world in which 06 would live willingly.

If he were a praying sort of person, he'd be praying now. That 06 would assume the obvious—he was ambushed in his sleep, tranquilized, hauled deadweight home to HQ—and not ask him point-blank how it played out. The lie he's already told her feels like a solid object lodged in his throat, halfway swallowed. But it hurts less than it did. Tomorrow, provided he makes it through the last dregs of the night, it will hurt less still. Which scares him almost worse than the prospect of her questions.

But she's not hurt. That's the main thing. They'll regroup, bide their time a little, try again when the moment is right.

Which brings him up against the third and maybe worst thought he's avoiding.

They could have run farther. Run smarter. Changed their location as soon as their food had been stolen, the container obviously compromised. Destroyed the Director's weird tech toy before it got a word out. Done literally any number of things in any number of ways better.

What he's desperately trying not to wonder now is: if he could make all those choices over, would he have chosen any differently?

He doesn't know how to explain this to 06 either, this hesitation. It's not like he *enjoys* it here. But he's not strong like 06, not brave like 06, at least not in the same way. Not in a way that here, now, embedded in the fever like a fly in amber, he can begin to recognize, let alone articulate. If they are halves of a whole, he and she, they are not symmetrical. They complement. It is because their jagged places slot together so exactly that they are so well and thoroughly enmeshed.

If she is the blade that holds the blood in, then he is the wound that endures.

He moves the vast weight of his head, trying to ignore how the room swings and settles around him, and glances at the next cot over.

And finds 06 staring back. She's reclined at the precise angle that won't trip the sensors arrayed around her cot (she's demonstrably a flight risk; the Director is a learning creature; the second 06 so much as sits up to stretch her arms, there'll be alarms, sentry bots, more tranquilizers, etc.) and holding that position, uncomfortable as it looks, while keeping 22's readout display in clear view. Half-delirious as he may be, 22 knows to his marrow that he is being sat vigil over. That her stillness is only partly so as not to wake him. She's hungover on whatever she's been shot up with, and she's conserving energy. He has the distinct impression that if Death itself came for him on this cot, it would end up with 06's teeth in its throat.

"I thought you were asleep," 06 whispers.

"I thought you were," 22 whispers back.

She shakes her head, infinitesimally, and winces. "Are you okay?"

Is he okay. No, he is not okay. On almost every conceivable level, he is a very far cry indeed from okay.

"Yeah," he says. "Are you?"

"I guess." She sighs. "Just pissed off."

Invisibly, 22 braces. But:

"I messed up," she says. "I shouldn't have left you there alone. You're sick. You couldn't defend yourself. It was stupid."

For a moment she looks like the alarm sensors are the only thing keeping her from picking up this whole building and dropkicking it into low orbit. Then it passes and she just looks dejected. It's such an alien expression on her face that 22 opens his mouth to tell her the truth.

He'll have to tell her someday, he knows. Better to get out in front of it before the Director breaks her promise and does it for him. Make it look less like betrayal than she will. Which isn't another lie, exactly, but also kind of is. The fact that he's only trying to protect her does not make one iota of difference in the lightening of that burden. He will live out his life in this building with the weight of it around his neck.

In the morning he'll reach into his pocket and find a wad of bills, neatly folded, and a note written on what looks like receipt paper in the childish scrawl of something unused to holding a pen, reading: *next time don't let me catch you.* He'll look around, for what he isn't sure—a tiny floating octopus? an ultraviolet fog? a tiny 06?—but there's nothing. He'll glance up at the ceiling vent, certain for a second that he made out movement there, and then it will be gone, and was probably just the fever anyway.

Next time he won't—in fact he'll never see the probe array again, or at least won't recognize it if he does—but it won't matter then either. Or the next time. Or the next.

Looking across four feet of empty space at each other, both children realize simultaneously: the only reason they're here right now is because they were trying to save each other. Their best chance of escape is alone. Untethered. Broken back down to halves. Time would smooth their edges. It's the only way they'll make it out alive.

It's realized simultaneously, and simultaneously discarded. Neither of them does the thought the dignity of so much as mentioning it aloud.

"We'll do better next time," he tells her.

"Next time," she agrees, and her nod is a blood pact, is his doom. As he is hers, today and tomorrow and forever. They can't quite see the future's shape from here, but they can feel its waiting presence. Each suspects, in their own way, that it will not have to wait for long.

For now 22 nods back, and 06 finally lets herself relax against the crappy pillow, and the future is pushed back at the rate of one second per second, and barreling toward them at the same, but for now it feels a little farther off, somehow.

AFTERWORD

THESE ARE ALWAYS fun to write because the process from project to project is always so different. In this case, the story fell on me out of nowhere. I have a bit of a, um, history with writing what I think at the time are stand-alone books (in this case, *Firebreak*) that then go on to accrue More Material because the characters refuse to be evicted from my head to make room for the characters of whatever it is I'm supposed to be working on next. While *Firebreak* will never turn into a duology or trilogy or series, this isn't even my first foray into writing side adventures for operatives 06 and 22.

This one started for the same reason most of my projects start: because my process is pure chaos. Some random thought will bounce around awhile until it glues itself onto another totally unrelated random thought, and then another one will join the party, and suddenly I have the plot for a book. At least this time it didn't involve zip-tying three genres together.

I had already written a novelette where 06 and 22 are fifteen years old and ridiculous ("Pathfinding!", which you can find over at *Uncanny*, if so inclined) but I wanted to write them younger. I don't know why, except I wanted to take a look at them at an age when their reprogramming isn't yet complete (if it ever is) and their memories of their old lives can still be accessed, if patchily, like a fading dream you claw after scraps of.

What this glued itself to, hilariously, was random nostalgia for one of my favorite books when I was five or so—*The Boxcar Children* by Gertrude Chandler Warner. I gave it a reread for the first time since I was a kid and was struck by a few things, namely the antiquated gender norms—the oldest boy is the only one who leaves the woods, finds work, procures food and supplies, interacts with people, etc., while the two girls stay behind and cook and clean and take care of their little brother—the total focus on work ethic, and how this still managed to make complete sense to me as a child who hated chores, because what these kids were doing, while *still chores*, were done *on their own terms to meet their own goals*; and how the book was written in a time when all kinds of things could be found by the children in the local junkyard and repurposed, because they were made of materials that lasted. I immediately started wondering how that kind of story would transpose to a setting where nothing is built to last and most everything is low-quality, plastic, disposable. A world of planned obsolescence and single use. I mean, we're pretty much living there now, but I realized I already have a setting where this is even more true: the supercity of New Liberty in the first quarter of the twenty-second century, literally owned—like the rest of America—by corporations.

After that, it just all fell together. It was supposed to be a light fluffy piece about 06 and 22 running off to have a (mis)adventure in the nearest thing to an abandoned boxcar they seemed likely to find, enjoying an independence and freedom they don't exactly tend to experience in the Stellaxis basement, and the Director trying, and mostly failing, to get them to come "home." I also deeply enjoy leaving little Easter eggs for my regular readers, so the mothballed probe array that the Director recruits and is in the end outsmarted by is SABRINA, the Semi-Autonomous Bio-Reconnoitering Intelligent Nanobot Array from my middle-grade novel *Jillian vs Parasite Planet*, and there are all kinds of little callbacks throughout to both *Firebreak* and "Pathfinding!" and probably some of my other stuff because that's how I amuse myself (and hopefully at least two or three readers).

What I wasn't expecting was for this story to do so much totally unplanned for character work heavy lifting. I thought I was writing a cozy little adventure and ended up with a whole tragic underpinning for basically everything 22 does throughout the course of *Firebreak*. Without spoilers for those of you who haven't read that yet, here in that shipping container is where the seed for his long game is planted. I wasn't expecting that. But I've always found that to be the fun part of writing—not the stuff you plan out, but the stuff that evolves or appears out of nowhere, materializing to land at your feet, in a way that sometimes you don't even notice until the whole thing is written and you go back and read it over like *where on earth did this come from?* For my money, that's where the good stuff lives.

NICOLE KORNHER-STACE is the author of the Norton Award finalist *Archivist Wasp* and its sequel, *Latchkey*. Her short fiction has appeared in *Uncanny*, *Clarkesworld*, *Fantasy Magazine*, and many anthologies. Her latest books are the adult SFF thriller *Firebreak* (Saga Press, 2021) and middle-grade space adventure *Jillian vs Parasite Planet* (Tachyon Publications, 2021). She lives in New Paltz, NY, with her family. Kornher-Stace can be found online on Twitter @wirewalking.